The Frightened Valley

On their arrival in Elk Valley, Lenny and Rio Sand are immediately faced with the oppressive force of the great JUG Ranch. The greedy owner, James Umac Genner wants the brothers' land; and his foreman, Pike Branca, wants Lenny's fine Moro stallion for himself. When the mysterious Amy Teague arrives from San Francisco, it isn't long before Branca decides that he wants her too.

The valley is primed for trouble and ready to explode and when tensions reach breaking point, the JUG aggressors decide that it is time to claim everything. But there are other people involved and some will be torn apart when the time comes to decide where loyalty ends and betrayal begins.

Gathered together at Amy Teague's ranch along Plum Creek, family and friends struggle for their survival in an inescapable gun battle.

The Frightened Valley

ABE DANCER

A Black Horse Western

ROBERT HALE · LONDON

Typeset by
Derek Doyle & Associates, Liverpool.
Printed and bound in Great Britain by
Antony Rowe Limited, Wiltshire.

1
Elk Valley

Nestled in the foothills of the Baldy Mountains, miles from the railhead at Butte, Elk Valley lay secluded and beautiful. It was unspoiled cattle country in which the JUG ranch spread across 250,000 fertile acres.

The land broke up naturally into crop fields, woods and pasture land. The ranch house lay to the south, with outhouses and barns to the north. The land shelved to a willow-bordered stream that ran from west to east and the grazing began beyond the stream. The higher north-western corner of JUG consisted of thousands of acres of bigtooth maple and pine which were cut for fuel and building. The trees ran all the way to Big Soak, a fish-filled lake from which springs trickled down to join the stream. The eastern border was more hostile; marshland infested with snappers and buzzworms.

JUG's owner dominated the valley and the small town of Fishtail, ran it with a formidable oppression. James Umac Genner was a big man, caught in the set of middle age. He had enormous, strong hands, a stubble of grey hair that matched the colour of his eyes and he wore black suits.

Because of the Jude Basin that separated Fishtail from the state seat of Billings, Sheriff Porton Gane had been glad to deputize James Genner. Over a period of time, he'd virtually handed over that remote section of Montana territory.

But ten years ago, Genner had been little more than a landscalper. He'd staked a line of claims along the Elk Valley, then sold them on to settlers who were never going to make it across the Rockies.

There was no trouble though; there was private law. After breaking the land of a broad and bountiful valley, the homesteaders were trapped, eking out an existence at Genner's benefaction. That he might be feared as well as despised was a possibility to which Genner was wholly indifferent.

There had never been any challenge to his rule – his megalomania – until the day Lenny and Rio Sand rode into the valley.

The brothers arrived during the water-blue of first dark. Riding behind three pack-ponies, Lenny was mounted on his moro stallion. Behind him followed a team of bays, pulling a freight wagon. Perched on the high seat, holding the lines, sat Rio. From beneath a battered slouch hat, long dark hair brushed the shoulders of his skin coat.

They made no halt in Fishtail. They walked straight down its single street of weather-beaten buildings. Early lights bloomed through open doorways, through windows coated with dust. A few townsfolk watched, half interested, from the boardwalks, one or two remained until the short train had moved out from the end of town.

After a few minutes, Lenny dropped back to ride beside the wagon.

'Ain't changed a lot, Rio,' he said. 'Could've been yesterday I passed through here, instead of six years ago. Elk Valley ain't changed with the times.' Lenny threw a short backward glance at the town. 'Just as well though . . . we'd have lost our land file. It would have been taken up long ago.'

Rio stared ahead, into the distance. 'You were right about the valley, Lenny,' he said. 'It sure looks like that Eden Pa was always talkin' about.'

A smile slowly creased Lenny's sunburned features. 'Yeah, but don't forget this James Genner. Apparently he's had a grip on this valley for a decade . . . an' everyone in it. He don't welcome strangers with open arms.'

'Very shortly he'll discover his luck's run out. Pa always said, if you've got land you've got war.' Rio squinted into the approaching darkness. 'Looks like someone comin'. He laughed. 'Maybe it's the welcomin' party.' He called softly to the bays and hitched the lines, reached for his .44 revolver.

But Lenny displayed little of his brother's enthusiasm for chance. Cautiously he watched the rider draw close. In the fading light, he saw him run his eyes searchingly over the wagon and pack-ponies.

As the man pulled in, Lenny saw the monied trimmings; tooled saddle, latigo boots, caught the gleam of a plated Colt.

'Looks like you fellers're totin' some stuff there. Aimin' to settle hereabouts?' the man asked offhandedly. But before Lenny or Rio answered, he continued a touch plainer. 'You'll be needin' to see James Genner. He controls just about everythin' here in the valley . . . everythin' except me that is. I'm Pike Branca.'

Branca then took notice of Lenny's horse, missed the
weary glance the brothers exchanged. He tipped a pale-
coloured Stetson up from his forehead. 'That's a fine
lookin' bronc you're ridin' feller. Looks a little hot-
blooded for farmin'. You'll be wantin' to sell. I'll take
him off you for a fair price.'

Lenny looked from Branca to his brother. With a
sigh he shook his head. 'I appreciate your eye an' your
interest, but the horse ain't for sale.' He leaned
forward, ran his fingers through the stallion's dark
mane.

A flash of irritation showed suddenly in Branca's
face. 'My horse an' fifty dollars. That's the best offer
you'll get around here.'

Lenny swore silently, under his breath. 'When this
horse comes up for sale, I'll hang a sign around its
neck. But right now it ain't. Not to you or anyone else.
Now if you don't mind—'

'A hundred dollars,' Branca threw in.

Lenny backed off the stallion a few short steps. He
caught the trace of intolerance in Branca's voice and
threateningly touched the grip of his own .44 Colt.

'Race him. Race him against my dun. I'll bet you the
hundred dollars.' Branca flung out the challenge as if
he thought Lenny was interested – on the hook.

Lenny nudged the moro forward again, rubbed up
close to Branca's mount. 'If it wasn't quite so dark, I'd
be able to see if you were as stupid as you sound,
cowboy,' he said calmly. He noticed with concern the
glint of wildness in Branca's eyes.

'I ain't forgetin' you, stranger. You'll be gettin' a
piece a land that ain't fit for spittin' on,' Branca
sneered.

Rio clicked the bays forward. 'Us dirt farmers have

got our land, an' it's been filed an' paid for,' he yelled angrily at Branca. 'It'll be christened Woodside, an' it's along Plum Creek, so we won't be callin' on you or Mr Genner. Now get out of our way, you ugly son of a bitch, or I'll run you down.'

The blood raced in Pike Branca. Self-control wasn't one of his strong points and Lenny had anticipated the man's abrupt response.

He nudged hard at the moro's flanks as Branca flourished the quirt he carried in his right hand. The stallion lunged, his muscled shoulder piling into the dun. The animal shivered with the impact, went down to its knees. For a second or two it struggled silently in the dirt before lurching back to its feet.

Branca was shaken, clutching firmly at the saddle horn. When he straightened he was looking into a long-barrelled six-gun.

'I'm gettin' real irritated by your manner, cowboy,' Lenny snapped. 'Now, if I have to pistol-whip you to shut you up, then I will.' Lenny turned the Colt, grip forward, barrel running down his forearm. 'Me an' my brother here had hoped to be at the creek before mornin' . . . so git.' He slammed the frame of the gun against the dun's rump, pulled back as the horse and rider bolted forward.

'I think I'm gonna like Elk Valley brother . . . ain't been a dull moment since we got here,' Rio chuckled.

'A promising party,' said Lenny with imused irony. 'This time tomorrow, we'll probably be tryin' to outrun bullets.'

Rio picked up the lines. 'Let's went,' he called to the bays, shouted at Lenny. 'Why didn't you race him? You coulda turned that dun barn sour, an' you know it.'

Lenny pushed the Colt back into his holster. 'Not

you as well, Rio,' he said falsely bothered. 'The moro's a fine piece o' horse flesh, but if you were willin' to bet a hundred dollars your horse was faster, what the hell would you be wantin' to exchange it for?'

'Right . . . I was just askin'?' Rio said uncertainly.

Lenny hadn't got it quite right about the trouble. Out at the JUG, James Genner indulged Branca's tirade against the Sand brothers. But the rancher sounded secure, was in no hurry to react over two strangers, however galling to his long-time foreman.

'If the land *does* belong to them . . .' he started to say, staring thoughtfully out into the night. 'However, you don't normally see settlers ridin' bloodstock. We'll keep an eye on 'em, Pike . . . just in case,' he conceded.

Before the first white tendrils of frost touched the valley, Lenny and Rio Sand had fashioned a snug, if rudimentary, cabin. They worked through the depths of winter, learned to understand and value the land, wore the mantle of drifters who'd found home.

For a few months the brothers were at ease, undisturbed. Spring created its magic, and the streams ran wild with melt water, The pasture was green again and trees were budding when Amelia Teague and Dub Horley arrived in Fishtail.

2
Town Shooting

Like Lenny Sand, nobody knew where she'd come from, only that she came in on the once-a-week coach from Butte. Early evening found her standing outside the stage office, gripping the hand of a two-year-old boy. They gazed up at the immense Montana sky, totally innocent of the stir their arrival had caused.

Amelia Teague was taller than average. She had a small pointed chin and a square jaw. Her eyes were pale blue, and below a coiled crown of red hair, her skin was fine; a feature she carefully guarded with a bonnet and veil against Fishtail's rare weather.

It was a long minute before she realized she was being stared at, before she met the eyes of curious onlookers. For a while she stood matching their gaze, then she tugged at the child's cap. When she lifted him, the small crowd shuffled uneasily and she turned away.

Lenny Sand was kicking his heels. Until the incoming mail was sorted, he was talking with Ben Chawkin the proprietor of the Silver Grass Hotel. When Amy Teague walked in he turned his head and stared, took a step back and lifted his hat. Their eyes met as she stood the child in front of her and Lenny smiled, nodded a welcome.

Without a word the lady stepped across the reception area to sign the register. As she wrote, Pike Branca pushed open the front door of the hotel. He stopped and looked straight ahead, fixed his eyes on Amy.

'It's quiet at the moment, Mrs Teague. You've got yourself a nice room,' Chawkin said, watching the lady place the pen back in its pot.

'Thank you,' she said, 'but I'm *Miss* Teague. And my nephew here's Dub Horley.'

Chawkin's enquiring eyes took in the child, 'Yes ma'am . . . Dub Horley,' he echoed. He took a key from the desk and, guessing the lady's luggage was still on the sidewalk, walked towards the door.

When Pike Branca moved aside, Lenny caught the expression on his face. As the man looked after the girl, Lenny remembered the look. It was avarice, similar to that he'd affected when he saw the moro.

Unaware of Lenny's presence, the JUG foreman suddenly turned and left the hotel. Lenny delayed his own leaving a moment then followed to the street. He drove his team and wagon to the livery and got them stabled for the night, Later, he too signed for a room at the Silver Grass. He read the name above his own signature.

'Amelia Teague. San Francisco'.

It was nearly time for the evening meal when she showed again. She had a word with Chawkin, asked for a tray of food to take to her room.

She waited for a few minutes by the register desk, then thanked the girl who brought out the food. As she turned to the stairs, Pike Branca rose from his chair at the end of the long dining-table.

'I'll carry that, ma'am,' he called to her. 'Wouldn't want you to fall.'

Amy Teague looked at him unsmiling. 'It's a food tray . . . I can manage, thank you,' she said.

Lenny's shoulders heaved as he bent to his eating, as Elk Valley's would-be Lothario stared around him foolishly. Sniggers sounded from the table but were quickly stifled when Branca turned. Forgoing the apple-pie and cream, he wasn't long in leaving the hotel.

'Won't seem so bad after he's swallowed the Bear Pit,' Lenny said understandingly.

Branca didn't return to the hotel until the following morning. Lenny was standing on the veranda, building a smoke, when the JUG foreman appeared. Although the man's eyes were bleary, red-rimmed as a result of his night in the Bear Pit saloon, he was dressed in a fancy shirt and waistcoat.

When he saw Lenny, a scowl creased his raw-looking features. 'Decided to sell the moro yet?' he grated.

For six months or more, the asking had been Pike Branca's repeated greeting, and it stirred up a tetchy response from Lenny.

'I dunno which part of "no" you don't understand, Branca, an' it's makin' you a tiresome son of a bitch. If I do ever decide to sell, you'll be the last to know,' he said.

Branca sniffed hard, winced at the instant headache. 'I usually get what I want, Sand.'

Lenny said nothing. He lit his cigarette, flipped the spent match into the street.

As always his unaffected manner nipped at Branca's own disposition.

'You're gonna get burned, feller,' the foreman

sniped, his voice still thick with the roughness of sleep.

Lenny gave a short laugh. 'Seems to me, you're the one's doin' the burnin' up with wantin',' he goaded.

For a moment Branca stared at him, puzzled. 'If you mean what I think. . . .'

The appearance of Amy Teague on the sidewalk stopped Branca and his threatening reply, but his colour had improved.

Miss Teague was leading her nephew by the hand, With a forefinger, Lenny touched the brim of his hat and nodded briefly, stepped aside. From the street, Branca hesitated, self-consciously held up an acknowledging hand.

As the young lady approached the corner of the hotel, the old swamper, Smiles Macaw, stepped hesitantly from the narrow alleyway between it and the next building. Looking up and seeing someone he was about to collide with, he stumbled. Amy Teague flinched and, gripping the child, withdrew a step. But Macaw was still cut with the night drink and made no obvious effort to avoid her. He focused uncertainly, held out dirt-stained fingers that touched her arm.

It was an instinctive, guileless act, but in Pike Branca's mind it was the chance he was looking for, the opportunity to get his name wrote up on Amelia Teague's dance-card. He rushed at Macaw, and before anyone could follow what was happening, he'd seized the old man with one hand and was slapping his whiskered face with the other.

'You crazy old drunk,' he raged, 'laying your filthy paws on a lady. Perhaps this'll teach you.'

Macaw staggered backward. He buckled, but kept his feet beneath him. His face was puffy and red-mottled and a trickle of blood appeared from a split lip.

'No . . . please stop,' the lady protested, drawing the child closer.

But it had no effect. In Macaw's befuddled brain only one thing registered. He'd been pushed around, slapped into humiliation. Mumbling incoherently, he reached for the waistband of his trousers, dragged clumsily at the butt of an ancient Paterson Belt pistol.

Pike Branca wasn't to be sidetracked either. In the morning light his Colt glinted as he pulled the trigger.

Macaw was still dragging stubbornly at his gun as he was hit. Branca's bullet had shattered his chest and he crumpled, fell without a further sound into the hard-packed soil.

Amy Teague was struck with revulsion as she stared at the pathetic looking body of Smiles Macaw. Lenny was angry at knowing he'd witnessed a cowardly, cruel murder. He'd spent enough time in Fishtail to know that Smiles Macaw was one of its most harmless characters. A pathetic drunk, the gun he carried was nothing more than a seized-up keepsake from a distant war.

A group of men hurried along the street. Without saying anything, one of them kneeled to withdraw the pistol from Macaw's lifeless grasp. He worked at the stiff action and displayed the empty cylinder, held it up for all to see.

Branca's face drained as he realized the implication. 'Why'd he make a grab for it, if it wasn't loaded? How was I to know?' he bristled, but was worried and defensive.

Lenny was watching Amy Teague. Her nephew was staring up around him at the confusion and noise. He whimpered and she stooped to pick him up.

Before anyone had time to respond to the shooting, a small, bent stick of a woman came rushing from the alleyway. In her haste, her eyes fixed on Macaw, she almost tripped to fall alongside him. She made guttural sounds in her throat, tugged at him, rolled and pushed his body.

Miss Teague put Dub back down; the movement caught the old woman's attention.

She looked up, her face sallow and withered. 'It was 'cause o' you.' She almost spat the words at Miss Teague. 'I seen it . . . it was you . . . you killed him,' she sobbed, near to breakdown.

The drama held everyone. Branca, who had replaced his gun in its holster, was eyeing the small gathered crowd. He was scared, but at the same time relieved to have the attention diverted.

There were a few more moments of distressing silence, and then Miss Teague turned away. Holding Dub tight against her, she slowly stepped the few paces back to the hotel entrance.

She glanced at Lenny as she passed by, and he almost reached out to give her reassurance. He cursed bitterly under his breath, looked back to the group of people in the street.

Allie Macaw had been helped to her feet, and she turned stiffly to face Branca. What she had to say sickened Lenny.

'I'm not blamin' you, Mr Branca,' she said, sniffling. 'I told him . . . told him that one day that stupid ol' cannon would be the death of him.'

Nervous sweat ran down Branca's face and he gulped, nodded. 'We'll take him inside,' he muttered to two men who'd arrived along the sidewalk.

They were JUG punchers, and as they indolently picked up the wretched body of Smiles Macaw Lenny felt anger and revulsion for Pike Branca, felt the bile rise in his throat.

There would be a hearing, but Lenny knew that Branca would evade any meaningful law process because he carried the protection of James Genner – and in Fishtail, Genner *was* the law.

But Lenny's rope was being coiled. He knew that an open shoot between the JUG spread and the Sand brothers wasn't too far off.

3
The Involvement

Fights were hardly unique in Fishtail. Killings were
infrequent, and usually the result of long-time grudges.
Had the recent shooting involved anyone other than
Macaw and Branca, it would have been talked about for
a short while, then forgotten. Had it been a stranger
even, it wouldn't have earned much more than a bone-
yard footnote.

But Allie Macaw had been right. By always carrying
the antique weapon, Smiles Macaw had finally and
fatally tempted fate. The trouble was the old swamper's
routine was well known – even to Pike Branca.

In small groups, the townsfolk talked out their bad
feelings. In the Bear Pit, Lenny Sand overheard
rumblings that would have unsettled Branca. He also
noticed that some JUG riders were avoiding town
because of their displeasure.

Early one morning he noticed that two riders left
town; one rode into the valley towards the JUG, the
other headed across the Jude Basin in the direction of
Billings. He smiled ironically when he was told that
neither of them were James Genner's men.

Lenny decided to stay on in town for a while, await an outcome. So far as he knew, there'd only been three witnesses to the shooting – Amelia Teague, Allie Macaw and himself as well as little Dub. But most lawful procedures were left to Genner. Lenny wondered if he'd be called upon to testify – doubted it.

As time dragged by he considered going home, turning his back on something that didn't have to be his business. That's what his brother would tell him. He hardly spoke to a soul, thought it was because of the rancour between him and the JUG foreman. But he knew it wasn't that. It was because he was a witness, knew the truth of Smiles Macaw's death. There were many townsfolk that would worry about the style and scope of Genner revenge if Lenny Sand gave his evidence.

Elk Valley was filled with a deep-red flush of light when the JUG party rode into Fishtail. With his head lowered against the dipping sun, Lenny was sitting outside the grub house.

He reached for his makings, made a cigarette to conceal his interest. There were eight riders, six of them in from the home range.

'Appealing company,' murmured Lenny as he watched James Genner leading them in.

As they swept past, Genner saw Lenny. He was riding a light rig, his big hands expertly jiggling the reins of a gleaming black mare. Alongside him rode a boy with the same confident bearing. He wore buckskins and a Stetson atop his unusually long curly hair. Lenny recognized him as Huck Genner – the son.

He sat covertly watching, until the riders made the big corral adjoining the livery stable. Then he walked across the street, proposing to have a chat with Ben

Chawkin before turning in early. On those rare nights when the JUG outfit was in town, he knew that to wander too freely abroad was asking for trouble, as good as incitement.

When he got to the hotel, the lamps in their sconces were unlighted and the lobby and dining-room were bleak and gloomy. Puzzled, he pulled a rocker over to one of the front windows, and made another cigarette. As he smoked, he thought maybe, just maybe, Amy Teague was around.

He thought about her for a while, not for the first time wondered what she was doing in Fishtail, how long she'd stay. She didn't seem to have any friends or family, even acquaintances in the valley.

It was the sound of the bell above the front door that interrupted his thinking. He opened his eyes, looked up to see Huck Genner closing the door behind him.

He'd seen the lad a few times before, but always at a distance. Now from half a dozen paces he saw how slight he was. In the skin outfit, and with his locks, Lenny thought he looked more like a young woman standing in the shadows.

As the boy peered across the room, Chawkin suddenly appeared from his office.

'Young Huck,' he said. 'Good evening.' He appeared to be cheery and went over to light the lamps.

Huck smiled a greeting and raised his hand. As the light grew he looked around. He saw Lenny and his gaze faltered momentarily. 'I'd like one of Pa's rooms, Ben,' he said to Chawkin.

Chawkin looked curiously bothered. Most likely because James Genner retained some rooms exclusively for JUG use. 'They're all taken, Huck. There's been a lot of you in town,' he said almost apologetically.

The youngster didn't seem put out, thought for a few seconds. 'Pike's in town for a few days, he has a room, hasn't he?' he said. '*I'll* take it. He won't mind. He can sleep in the livery stable with the boys.'

Chawkin was worried about observing the pecking order. 'Yeah, he might well of been there last night . . . didn't show up here,' he answered half-heartedly.

'Probably drunker'n a skunk,' Huck shrugged. 'Oh well, there's always more room outside than in. I'll just bed down under the sidewalk, Ben . . . ask the rats to move over.'

Chawkin's mouth opened and his eyes rolled, as Huck turned away. He knew he was being joshed, but he thought on what Huck's father would have to say. 'Mr Huck . . .' he started.

'Give him my room,' Lenny interrupted.

Chawkin smiled, winked at Lenny. 'There,' he said with genuine relief. 'Who said a kindness never got beyond the Mason–Dixon Line?'

'My pa,' Huck quipped, turned to face Lenny.

Clutching his Stetson, the Genner boy was aware that Lenny was curiously watching him. He met his gaze with open and equal interest.

'You're Lenny Sand, aren't you . . . friend of Pike Branca,' he said, smiling mischievously. 'Not everyone at JUG's unfriendly . . . there's a bunch a' rattlers out on the marshes.' He hesitated for a moment. 'Seriously, Mr Sand, can I talk to you a moment . . . privately?'

Lenny was intrigued by the boy's openness. He nodded, indicated the other side of the room, away from the interested Chawkin. He pulled up a chair which Huck waved away.

'The rider who came out to the ranch to see Pa,' he began immediately. 'He said that you and the girl who came in on the Butte stage were the only ones who saw the shooting. Is that right?'

Lenny didn't answer immediately. He was wondering at the purpose of the question; why Huck didn't ask Branca? But he thought he knew the answer to that. It was the follow-up question that made sense of it.

'Was Pike . . . Mr Branca . . . had he been drinking?'

Lenny saw the unmistakable trace of feeling. The boy was looking for something.

'I'm sorry, Genner, he was cold sober. It *was* close to midday . . . and Macaw's wife also saw the shooting.' Lenny felt as if he had to press on. 'I'm sorry . . . I don't understand, If he'd been drunk . . . it would have made some difference? Been OK?' he questioned.

'I didn't mean that,' Huck replied quickly, but Lenny saw that he did.

'Was it true,' he sounded a bit uncertain now, erratic, 'that this girl . . . Miss Teague . . . provoked Smiles's attention . . . goaded Pike to . . . intervene?'

Lenny felt angry at the obvious attempt to bend the truth, the Genner pressure. 'Only in as much as your attempt to provoke *me*,' he snapped.

Before Huck responded he carried on, 'Contrary to what you might have heard,' he said coldly, 'Miss Teague was simply mindin' her own. She's hardly the painted cat. She was with the kid . . . he's no more'n a button. Old Smiles Macaw just bumped her . . . doubt if he even saw her. *He* was the one who was blind drunk. It was as close to murder as you'll ever get.' Lenny swallowed hard. 'You an' your pa got yourselves a real champion in Pike Branca, Mr Genner.'

Huck balled his fists and stared up at him. As Lenny had intended, he was taken aback and uncomfortable.

'But don't worry,' Lenny ended cynically. 'What I saw

. . . any evidence I might give, don't amount to a hill a' beans I reckon. Not here in Fishtail.'

Huck Genner seemed not to have heard. He mumbled something about Pike probably not being bothered either way, but Lenny didn't want to hear it.

'I'll not waste any more of your time, Mr Sand,' he said quietly. 'Thanks for the room. Goodnight.'

As Huck climbed the staircase, Lenny thought the youngster had had a good try.

Lenny stayed only long enough to share a quick whiskey with Chawkin. Using back alleys, carefully avoiding the main street, he made his way to the livery stable. He checked over his team and with a blanket from under the driving seat, rolled into a spread of hay for the night.

It was mid morning when the coroner arrived from Billings. He'd ridden in with the man who'd gone to fetch him. The two men, who were both powdered with alkali dust from the Jude Basin, rode straight to the jail. It was where Pike Branca was waiting with James Genner. The hearing was what a lot of townspeople had been waiting for, and the event brought them milling into the street.

An hour later the county official reappeared. He was escorted by Genner, Branca and six JUG cowboys. The group made their way to the newly constructed civic office, which was at the opposite end of the town from the corral and livery stable. By the time Lenny had made his way along the street, there was already an excited crowd that almost filled the pine-clad hall.

Lenny elbowed his way to be near the front of the hall. On a makeshift platform James Genner leaned forward in his chair. While he talked to the coroner his eyes moved restlessly over the gathering crowd. Just behind him and to one side, Pike Branca looked tense and ill at ease, flinched when he saw Lenny. It was a sign that Lenny wouldn't be a welcome contributor to the proceedings.

Amy Teague hadn't arrived, and Lenny wondered whether she'd been summoned. But after a minute or so, when the general hubbub suddenly became whispers, he looked across the room to see her walking slowly towards the platform.

She was alone as he'd expected, and he wondered about the child: who'd be looking out for him. She hesitated at the foot of the low platform and the coroner indicated one of three empty chairs. She appeared to be calm and composed as she nodded her thanks and took her seat. But Lenny could see her clasped hands, the nervous fidget of her thumbs.

On an impulse he stepped up to the platform and took a seat. James Genner looked to him for a sign of intent, but nothing was said. Another minute passed and Allie Macaw shuffled her way to the front. Tight-faced and glaring at Amy Teague she folded herself into the last chair. The coroner had a quick look at Genner and started to outline the day's session.

Lenny thought that what followed was pure theatre comedy, considering it was meant to be a legal investigation into a violent death.

The coroner called out the names of the men who'd been called as jurors. With a great deal of shuffling and muttering they clumped on to the platform to stand in a line, awkward and self-conscious.

There was no formal questioning, no inquiring into the tragedy. Versions of the actual shooting were subjective and brief. The only thing in common and without question was that Smiles Macaw got to lie dead in the street. But the coroner deemed the outcome sufficient and launched into his conclusion.

'It has become perfectly clear that . . .' he began in an appeasing tone.

They were the only words that Lenny picked up on, though. He got to his feet and threw a hostile glance at Genner and Branca. As he left the room he looked frustratedly at Amy Teague, then disappointedly at Allie Macaw.

On the sidewalk, a couple of old-timers were speculating on the events inside. 'What's happenin'?' one of them asked eagerly as Lenny slammed the door behind him.

'Self-defence . . . Branca walks free. Mrs Macaw don't say a word 'cause James Genner'll stuff her basket with enough greenbacks to keep her quiet. That's what'll be happenin'.'

'It's over? They done all that in there?' the second man asked uncertainly.

'They will have, Pop . . . they will have.' Lenny spat the prophetic words into the distance, guessed it was nearly noon.

4
Overdue

It was mid afternoon and Lenny was hungry. It was either too late or too early for the hotel and he made for the end-of-town grub house. Hot Mulligan with plenty of sourdough was the comfort feed he needed. He sat at a bench thinking, eating slow. He was long overdue at Woodside, knew that Rio would be champing at the bit. If he didn't return with the ranch supplies soon, his brother would be ahead of the hounds. But he was reluctant to go back directly. He didn't want to give the impression he was beat, not to the JUG outfit, and certainly not to Amy Teague.

An hour later he strolled along to the Bear Pit saloon. He took a pack of cards from the barman and played solitaire at a wall table. He stayed a further hour, then went to the livery stable. He was working on the harness, buckling a collar on one of the bays, when he heard voices from outside, near the corral.

'See for yourself, ma'am, I ain't got nothin', only a couple o' utilities. The doc's got the rig. I'd help if I could. I'm real sorry, ma'am.'

It was Esbert Twine the stable man. 'Do you mind me

askin' why you're wantin' to ride out to Meadow Ranch, Miss Teague?' he asked.

'I own it,' Amy Teague said simply. 'Me and Dub, we own everything . . . even the hardware. Naturally we're eager to go out there.'

'Yeah . . . you would be, ma'am,' Twine agreed hesitantly.

Lenny thought maybe his prospects weren't all that bad. There were some folk in Fishtail who wanted a church; a theatre even. Rio wanted a dance-hall. For Lenny, Amy Teague would do nicely. Meadow Ranch was five miles from Woodside. A fork of Plum Creek divided them, and only a rising tract of full-grown aspen closed down the view of one from the other.

Yeah, good, he was thinking, when Pike Branca's voice sliced through his musing.

'You own Jed Tibble's place? You musta bought it blind. What price you pay, ma'am?'

'That's a tactless question, Mr Branca.' Amy Teague was obviously surprised. 'You have a reason for asking?'

Lenny squeezed his eyes shut. That's it Branca, he sniggered in silence. Overwhelm her with frontier etiquette. Forget you shot down a harmless old man in front of her. He grinned and gently let the buckle strap dangle, walked quietly to be nearer the stable door.

Pike Branca didn't sound too disconcerted. 'It's to do with Tibble, ma'am,' he said. 'I think he crossed Mr Genner. Musta been somethin' bad. The boss didn't give him much time to get clear of the valley. It's a bit of a surprise . . . how Tibble's managed to sell up so quick.'

'Mr Tibble's squabble doesn't interest or bother me,' Amy said tersely.

Branca was piqued, and it sounded in his voice.

'Well, maybe it should,' he replied. 'No real rancher would be interested in that two-by-four oufit.'

Lenny edged closer to the doorway as Branca went on, 'If it's meat on the hoof you're interested in, Miss Teague, come visit the JUG . . . take your pick a' the best.'

Lenny swore silently at Branca's boorish innuendo. He held his breath, waiting for more, but when Amy spoke again, her voice had lost none of its reserve or its temper.

'You have a twin, Mr Branca. In case you didn't know, he's to be found in Butte. When I last saw him there, he was at rest on a butcher's slab with a half lemon wedged in his mouth.'

Lenny laughed. It was loud enough to get him noticed and he stepped outside. Twine had backed off, was tugging at the wheel of a pie buggy. To Lenny's surprise, the boy Dub was sitting in the dirt, prodding horse-apples with a willow switch.

'I think Miss Teague's too much of a lady to come straight out with it Branca,' he said. 'But there's nothin' to stop *me*. You're a pig, an' real ugly with it.'

Branca spun at Lenny. 'Well, lookee here . . . it's the meddlesome sodbuster,' he sneered.

Lenny came close to smiling. 'I can take you and the boy out to Meadow Ranch, miss,' he said calmly. 'I've got a team and wagon. I've spent long enough in town, an' it's no more'n a few miles out of my way.'

Then, Branca railed angrily. 'You're outa the way *now*, Sand. It's about time somebody headed off that long nose a' yours.'

Amy looked suddenly worried. 'I don't want there to be any more trouble on my account,' she said, the upset sounding in her voice.

Lenny was unbuckling his gunbelt. 'There won't be, miss . . . it'll all be on mine. If you could wait just a few more minutes . . . blow some dirt off the kid perhaps?'

Amy nibbled her lip, held out her hand towards Dub. Branca was glaring at Lenny, his face dark, contorted with anger.

Holding his gunbelt in one hand, Lenny indicated the livery stable with the other. His intentions were clear to Branca, and removing his own Colt, the JUG foreman followed inside. Lenny tossed his hat, gun and belt into the back of the wagon, led the team outside.

He told Twine to hold the horses. 'Shouldn't be long, Bert,' he said casually.

In the stable, Branca placed his gun atop a crate. The men were evenly matched, no more than a few pounds apart in weight and none in height. But Branca lacked restraint, and as always when his temper broke, his impulse was to hurt, preferably with his hands.

As Lenny approached, Branca dropped his right shoulder and lashed out. His fist struck home savagely and Lenny's head recoiled. The force of the blow was pulverizing and drove instant darkness into Lenny's focus. The stomach-churning feeling of collapse gripped him, but he shook it off to meet Branca's forward assault with a short solid hook.

The effect wasn't as Lenny had hoped, and Branca piled on into him. He was forced back, blocking some of the blows with his forearms. The blows jarred and hurt, and Lenny was losing his footing. He went down to one knee, and Branca jumped away; but only to let drive with a booted foot. The blow was intended to break Lenny's ribs, and would have, if it had landed square. Lenny rolled downward, caught Branca's heel. He surged back, jerking Branca to the floor.

The men rolled apart, got back to their feet. Lenny was breathing hard and sucking in great glugs of air, a trickle of blood spilling from his nose. He backed off from Branca's charge, throwing his fists in short chopping blows. Branca's head juddered at the force, but his legs held out, drove him on. He landed a heavy right, then a sharp hammer blow that dropped Lenny to the floor again.

As Branca came stomping in, Lenny saw the triumphant grin, knew there was no time left to draw out the fight. Avoiding Branca's lashing feet, he turned quickly, smashing into the wooden crate. He grabbed it, swung it in front of him as Branca pitched forward. He saw the nickel-plated Colt go flying across the stable as he fiercely jabbed the roughly nailed laths upward.

There was an immediate gush of blood from Branca's forehead. The man groaned and reeled dizzily, giving Lenny time to gain his feet. Lenny bobbed and weaved, awaiting Branca's charge. It came suddenly, Branca's flailing fists wildly trying to smash him, to make contact.

Lenny measured his swing, drove in fast and hard with his right hand. The shock of the blow jarred his shoulder, but together with Branca's forward rush it was the final punch.

Branca's eyes glazed and his legs wobbled doubtfully. He fell heavily to the ground and lay there face down, his body quivering, trying to shake itself up.

Lenny stepped away and licked his lips, wiped the blood across his face with the back of his hand. 'That's a piece a' work needed doin' real bad,' he snuffled.

Outside he pushed his head into the water-trough, pulled away spluttering and blinking. Amy Teague and the boy were standing in front of him. He eyed Dub.

'Men's stuff,' he said, with a painful-looking grin.

A tormented-looking smile crossed Amy's face. 'I'm obliged to you, Mr Sand,' she said . . . 'me and Dub.'

'It's Lenny.'

'I know. I'm Amy.'

Lenny ran his fingers through his hair. 'I know.' He laughed. 'If you've baggage to pick up, I'll be outside the hotel in fifteen minutes.'

5
Retaliation

Heading east, along the valley, Lenny Sand's wagon pulled up a long verdant slope. The blue-black bulk of the Baldy Mountains lay to the west, the highest peaks still white with the snow that would linger until midsummer. Around them, the land was cut with fast-running streams.

Similarly captivated by the landscape as she approached her ranch, it was some time before Amy spoke.

'There are some things don't seem important when you're surrounded by all this,' she said.

'Some *thing* in particular?' Lenny asked.

'Who's going to believe that Dub isn't *my* child?'

'Me for one . . . if it matters. I heard you tell Chawkin that he was your nephew. Pike Branca was there too, from what I recall.'

'Yes . . . well he *is* my nephew. He's the child of my dead sister, Freyer. His father is dead too. There's no other family. Just me and Dub.'

Lenny listened with concern and well-concealed interest.

'The woman . . . Allie Macaw,' Amy continued. 'I don't think she's going to talk me up. Most people think the worst. . ., and she's got cause.'

'No she hasn't, Amy, an' you know it: What was it somebody said about "letting those without sin"? Here in the valley, there won't be too many o' them.'

After a thoughtful silence, Lenny pointed to Woodside as the wagon topped the rise. Across the tops of the aspens, its clutch of buildings could just be seen.

Meadow Ranch lay ahead of them, and after another fifteen minutes Lenny walked the bays into the home pasture, through a kitchen garden. There was an assortment of barns, sheds and a corral. Just inside a gate that led to the small logged house there was a pond where a wood duck paddled weary circles.

As Lenny drew the wagon to a halt in the yard, he asked Amy what other animals had come with the price.

Amy laughed. 'A bunch of cattle, some saddle-brokes and a work team.'

'Me an' Rio can tally the cows for you. Help you clear up a bit if you like,' Lenny offered.

Amy was lifting Dub from the wagon. 'Haven't you enough to keep you busy at Woodside?' she asked.

'We've got a herd on its way up from the Wyoming–Colorado border. Until it gets here there's not a lot to do. That's why I spent so long in Fishtail . . . partly. Rio probably took to the sack the moment I left. I'll have to shake him out.'

'You're being most neighbourly, Lenny,' Amy said gratefully. 'There probably are one or two things I could use your help with. I'll need to get someone eventually, but for the time being, I'll stay small. We'll get by.'

Amy could see the doubtful look in Lenny's face. 'I was born . . . brought up on a ranch,' she told him.

'A ranch in Frisco?' Lenny said, unbelieving. 'You certainly don't look like a farm kid ma'am.' Lenny smiled, shook his head as he pulled down a leather-bound trunk.

Amy handed Dub a small valise. 'The top dressings come from San Francisco. That's where I've been for the past year. But I was born and raised in Nevada . . . near Carson City,' she said steadily. 'My father owned a big ranch. My sister and I were his only children. Freyer . . . she . . .'

Lenny lifted a hand to stop her. 'You don't have to explain to me,' he said drily. 'Not many do.'

Amy indicated that Dub take the valise towards the house, then she turned to Lenny, gave him a serious smile. 'That's because they're probably too busy pulling your fist from under their nose. Hear me out anyway,' she said.

'One Christmas, a near neighbour had kinfolk arrive from San Francisco. Freyer met and fell for one of them; Clarkson Chappey was his name. But Pa found out and tried to stop it. Freyer was so young . . . she went with him back to California. It broke Pa . . . he never spoke of her again. Two years later he died. As soon as I could, I went to look for my sister. It took me three months.

'Clarkson . . . Clark, had worked as mate on a schooner. It sailed between San Francisco and Los Angeles. There was a bad storm . . . off Point Lobos. The boat ran into rocks and he was drowned.'

At that point of the story, Amy suddenly stopped talking. She faltered for a moment, but then continued:

'Dub wasn't much more than a newborn. Freyer was given some money from the Seamen's Mission, but it wasn't much. She got ill, but was too proud to write home . . . to Father. I tended her all I could, but she got worse. I took her to a Monterey hospital . . . she died there of the fever. I couldn't . . . didn't want to go back to Carson City.'

There was a long moment, then Amy looked up at the sky. 'I decided to move east . . . bring Dub with me . . . I'd look after him,' she said quietly.

Her story was so open and unaffected that Lenny felt the lump in his throat.

'I didn't have to be told that story, Amy,' he said haltingly. 'But if you've no objections, I'll tell it to my brother. Might just stop him thinkin' you're some sort of Jezebel.'

'Mmmm, I'd be obliged,' Amy said, and it was from that moment that Lenny knew how much he liked her.

'The cattleman whom we bought the feeder steers from in Colorado is an old buddy. The stock'll be real quality,' he enthused. 'I think maybe some of the drovers'll want to stay on when they see this land . . . Elk Valley. You'll likely have an admiration society, Miss Teague.'

'After two months with a herd of cattle? I should hope so, Mr Sand.'

Lenny puffed his cheeks, fumbled for a smoke. With Dub scuttling around them, they had a quick look at the sheds and out buildings. Beyond the corral, a small compound held the few horses.

Amy grinned. 'There's at least *one* good mount,' she said, indicating a small grey with a dark mane and tail.

'Yeah, good choice,' Lenny said, as he flared a match along a bleached pole.

As the pale gold of the western sky deepened to orange, Lenny knew Amy Teague was watching. Probably still standing by the corral, maybe holding Dub's hand.

As the wagon pulled back up the slope he whistled tunelessly but cheerfully. Until now it had always been Rio who'd brought back news of exploit and incident – hearsay which he'd pass on with inimitable spicy humour. But this time it was Lenny with the tale to tell.

'Hey, take it easy,' he called. The eager bays were headed for home and his muscles bunched as he held back on the lines.

They were trotting down the eastern run of the slope, when from somewhere in the aspens, the sharp crack of a rifle split the still, evening air.

As the noise reverberated along the valley, Lenny felt the punch in his right side. A wave of instant sickness hit him, slammed him to the verge of blackout.

'Oh no,' he groaned, then shouted into the sky. 'You don't take well to a beatin', do you, Branca!'

He rolled off the high seat into the wagon box, as another shot rang out. He heard a tearing sound, knew the bullet had bit the side of the wagon. 'You hit me, you son of a bitch,' he shouted angrily.

Lenny turned on his side, saw the blood running from below his ribs and switched the lines to his left. He knew he had to get out of range. 'Run, Berry,' he called out, as a third bullet ripped through the planking inches from his face.

On the near side, Berry whinnied shrilly. Lenny guessed by the sudden swerve of the wagon that the horse had been hit. But then the team broke, moved, into a dead run down the slope. Lenny was being bashed around and the pain from his side was agonizing. He was losing his grip, the lines slipping from his fingers. He twisted, pushed his hand against his chest and rolled. Desperate to keep control, he held on to the traces, pinned them to the floor under his weight.

Another bullet tore low into the wagon box, badly hurting his fingers as he curled them beneath him.

'What the hell you want, Branca . . . can't you see I'm dead?' he ground out as his head hit the boards. Then it was night – deep sleep time, and he didn't hear or feel any more.

6
Shattered Peace

Within five minutes the wagon was out on level grassland; the bays in a panicky dash for Woodside. When
they got close, the team swerved wildly across the hard-
pummelled ground that fronted the Sand brothers'
cabin.

The snap and tear of strained traces and drumming
hoofs brought Rio running from the makeshift smithy.
He grabbed for the bridle of Berry, the wounded bay,
clung on as the frightened mare plunged and reared.
He got winded and his chest heaved as he was buffeted
against the animal's sweat-streaming shoulders. He dug
his heels into the ground, pulled the dark head down
under his arm. It took a long minute before Rio was
able to stand still. He breathed heavily, the bay's nostrils
quivering, puffing anxiously.

Holding the bridle in his left hand he took a pace
back, saw the blood that mingled with dark sweat; the
deep gash that ran from the heavy muscles of Berry's
chest.

With his free hand Rio grabbed out at the panel of
the wagon, drew himself in close. He hissed through his

teeth, swore horribly as he saw his brother lying face down among the flour-bags, tins and boxed supplies.

From beneath Lenny's body, blood pooled until it fell through the cracked boards of the wagon floor.

Still holding Berry's bridle, Rio pushed his fingertips up under his brother's chin, deep into his throat. 'Never done this before,' he said, as he felt what he recognized as a pulse.

He turned his gaze to the pair of bays. 'You're home, an' I'll see to your injuries in a while. I'm gonna let go,' he yelled. 'Cause a fuss an' I'll shoot the pair of you.'

He turned Lenny over, gently moved his arm away from his side. There was big bleeding but Rio could see the bullet had only made a flesh wound. It was somewhere else that looked bad. A bullet had ripped through the back of Lenny's left hand, and Rio recoiled at the shattered, bloodied mess.

He yelled, calling for Edwards, the ranch waddy. It had never been mentioned, but Rio guessed there'd been a record of medicine in Edwards' past. Amongst his grips he'd kept a black valise and he seemed to know about the workings of flesh and blood.

'Let's get him inside,' he shouted at Edwards. 'He's shot up bad . . . his hand's a mess, but it don't look like he's dyin' from it.' Rio pulled out the narrow tailgate and took hold of Lenny's pants around his boots. 'Whoever did the shootin' used enough bullets. You'd a thought they was tryin' to break up the wagon.'

As Rio reached for Lenny's shoulders his eyes made a slow search of the high ground. He looked along the wagon road, swept his gaze across the aspen tree-line.

A mile to the north, a disturbed eagle had risen vertically from the timber-line. It circled high, winged low, rose to circle again. No animal was likely to disturb the bird in its remote eyrie – but a man with a rifle might.

As Rio and Edwards carried Lenny to the cabin, Lenny grunted, grimaced with pain and his eyes opened.

'We'll get you inside, brother,' Rio said. 'Ed's gonna carry out some field surgery.'

'I can't feel my hand, Rio, where's it gone?' Lenny asked.

'It's still here, Lenny, but it don't look too pretty . . . took a bullet.'

As soon as they'd laid Lenny on his bed, Edwards went to the barn for his bag, 'I ain't got much, but it'll be better'n bear piss an' snake bones,' he said.

Rio was making a clean-up of the wound below Lenny's ribs when his brother groaned, twisted his head. The thrust of pain brought him back to full consciousness.

'What's happened, Rio? I can't feel a thing.'

'There's a lot o' your paw left on the bed of the wagon, Lenny. Ed's done some elegant doctorin' but you ain't gonna be joinin' any sewin'-bee.' He smiled warmly at his brother. 'Somethin' goin' on I should know about?'

'It's the ladies, Rio. They been givin' me trouble.'

'Ladies don't normally go breakin' up half o' Montana with a rifle . . . not even if they're from Fishtail.'

'There's one in particular that caused it. Amelia Teague . . . she's the new owner of Jed Tibble's place. That's where I've been . . . takin' her home . . . with the kid.'

Rio's eyes rolled in confusion and his jaw dropped. 'You got me beat, Lenny. But I'm sure there's some sense somewhere. Just talk until you fall asleep.'

While Rio prepared oil-lamps, Lenny recounted his exploits in Fishtail. Lacking detail, he gave a stumbling but intriguing account until pain and weariness wore him down. As he closed his eyes, fighting the trauma of shock, Rio spoke quietly.

'So we've got ourselves a new neighbour. You think she's her own man, Lenny?' he asked.

Lenny made a short coughing laugh. 'Yeah, I reckon she's that, Rio . . . knows about ranchin' too,' he managed. He stared blearily with half-open eyes. 'What you thinkin' brother?' he sighed.

'I'll tell you, Lenny. Just raise a hand if you think I'm wrong. If I'm right, you close down an' we'll talk later.' Rio threw a leg over the back of a chair and rested his chin on his hands. He watched Lenny's face closely as he spoke.

'James Genner . . . he won't make her life any easier. He'll feel Woodside an' the Meadows are irritations. He might worry about some o' the other ranchers linkin' arms . . . but I doubt it. They'll all listen to their women. The Macaw woman'll be puttin' the fee-faw-fum on this Amy Teague.'

Rio saw some endorsing movement in Lenny's face and he carried on. 'From what you've said Lenny, sounds like the only person who ain't tainted is the Genner boy, Huck. But he ain't likely to go up against his own pa.'

Rio deliberated a moment, then he squinted closely at his brother. 'There's nothin' Genner can touch us with, Lenny, and he knows it. You reckon it was Pike Branca that took those shots at you?'

'Not really. He was just someone I'd been mindful of. He wouldn't have been up to sittin' in a saddle, let alone focusin' a rifle.'

'Yeah, sure,' Rio said, forgetting Lenny's fight with the JUG foreman. 'I guess maybe I'd better ride over to the Meadow ranch. I'd like to see this new lady friend o' yours. But seriously, if it wasn't Branca who put bullets in you, who the hell was it . . . what the hell did they want? Ed'll keep an eye on you, I'll get over there now.'

Rio went to get Edwards who returned with his medicine bag and a pitcher of clean water.

'You ain't gonna die, brother,' Rio said. 'But that hand's gonna give you some cheerless moments. Ed says he'll tend to the fever when it hits you. When you're asleep he'll ride out . . . get some moss an' willow . . . make a poultice or somethin'.'

Rio nodded at Edwards, saw that Lenny had closed his eyes again. He opened the long drawer of the cabin table and quietly removed the big-gauge scatter-gun. Edwards nodded back at him.

Rio took a long, hard look at his brother, then flashed a portentous glance at Edwards. As Rio closed the door quietly behind him, the Woodside waddy felt the sickening liability of Lenny Sand's health clutch at his gut.

7
Marks of Guilt

Esbert Twine flicked water across Pike Branca's face until there was some response. He considered the full ladle. 'Musn't laugh . . . ain't funny,' he kept repeating to himself. He considered the consequences, thought of Smiles Macaw.

The crate had scarred Branca, but it was Lenny Sand's last punch that had shaped the damage. The man's right eye was swollen, closed tight, and split skin beneath the cheek-bone bloodied his swollen lips and chin.

As the crushed blood vessels made their massive bruising, Branca groaned. The pain and instinct for defence contracted his body, and he supported himself uneasily on an elbow.

'Did she go with him?' was his first demand of Esbert Twine.

Twine nodded hesitantly, and Branca muttered an oath. He grabbed for the dipper Twine was holding. He saw it was empty, cursed again and flung it across the stable.

'If you haven't thrown it all over me I'll drink some o' that. Get me some water, Scissorbill,' Branca snarled.

Twine did as he was told, then went out to the corral to rub down his plug work mares.

For a long time, Branca fussed over his cuts and bruises, but he didn't have much success in concealing them. Eventually he eased on his hat, and having picked up and cleaned his Colt, he walked from the stable. He stood in the open doorway for a moment, glad of the cool and the approaching dark.

'Find me Furloe Stilt. Try the Bear Pit. Tell him I want to see him right away,' he rasped at Twine. 'When you've told him, stay there – have a beer,' he added.

Glad of the respite, Twine hurried off along Fishtail's main street. It was only a short time later that Pike Branca was hugger-mugger with his top hand from JUG.

'Lenny Sand,' Branca ground out the name through his aching teeth. He was responding to Stilt's enquiry. 'Yeah, he surprised me, caught me on the turn. Otherwise . . .'

'Otherwise you'd o' skinned him,' Stilt completed Branca's flawed story.

'Yeah, it was over that Teague woman. He was makin' a play. Took her out to Meadow Ranch in his wagon. Had the kid along with 'em too.'

Stilt was uncertain about his summons. 'What is it you want of me, Pike? We can't do much if they've gone.'

A sudden surge of blood made Branca's head throb. 'Somewhere between here an' the ranch, you kill him, Furl. No warnin' an' no fancy wing-shootin',' Branca hissed. 'Then ride on to Woodside an' get me that moro stallion. Bring it back to JUG.'

Stilt kicked dirt with the toe of his boot. 'What about Sand's brother? He's likely to be around.'

Branca swore. 'Kill him too, if he gets in your way.'

'Yeah, if he gets *my* way. We're talkin' murder here, Pike. All over a woman an' a horse.'

'You know the JUG motto, Furl. "If you don't kill lice, they'll bite again".'

Stilt blinked his pale, humourless eyes. 'I'll need the light . . . better get goin'. See you back at JUG, Pike,' he said, as he unhitched his mount from a corral post.

Enduring the occasional rib-nudge, Branca followed Esbert Twine's tracks to the Bear Pit saloon. As he was about to push through the swing doors a voice called out his name. He turned to see a JUG puncher hurrying towards him.

Surprise flitted over the man's face, but knowing Branca's gift of striking out, no reference was made to the obvious beating.

'Been lookin' for you, Pike,' the puncher said. 'The old man wants to see you. He's at the agency.'

Branca grimaced when he entered the JUG cattle office and saw that Genner had his son with him. Huck was looking from a window out on to the street. He turned, but said nothing. His eyes were saying all he felt.

At his desk, Genner was equally silent, his weathered features unmoving. Defiantly, Branca met the scrutiny of the the rancher's calculating eyes, then with a nervy shrug he lowered himself into a chair.

Genner lifted a sheet of paper from his desk, and Branca looked to see what had been revealed. He shuddered, felt a wave of shock when he saw Smiles Macaw's cherished old Paterson Belt pistol.

Affected by a sense of accusation, he got back to his

feet. 'Is this supposed to mean somethin'?' he grated uneasily.

Genner's grey eyes moved again, swung upward. 'If the shoe fits, Pike . . .' He studied Branca's face. 'Meet up with one o' Macaw's family?' he asked acidly.

'If you've somethin' to say, boss, say it,' Branca replied shortly.

The tough rancher continued to eye him speculatively. 'I just did, Pike. Seems to me you've become somethin' of a liability.'

'What do you mean, "a liability"?'

Genner snapped back. 'If it had been anyone other than one o' my men that pulled that stunt with Macaw, they'd already be swingin' for Jesus, Pike, an' you know it.'

The severity of Genner's response rocked Branca.

Genner carried on. 'That old man hadn't packed a loaded gun for more'n twenty years. You're good enough with that shiny Colt o' yours . . . you could have hit him in the arm or leg . . . you'd have had the time.'

Branca started off on a lame excuse, a rejoinder, but thought better of it.

Genner nodded. 'Don't make it worse,' he said. 'For someone I've thought of as my own flesh and blood for all these years.' He shook his head sadly at the thought. 'Perhaps I should have listened,' he added enigmatically.

'The old fool was molestin' a lady . . . no tellin' what he might have done next.'

'So she's a lady now, is she? Not just a woman lookin' for "meat on the hoof"?' the old man said, sarcastically.

Branca's face coloured. 'Twine, eh? He came straight to you didn't he? I'll remember that.'

'You'll forget it,' Genner commanded. 'He's

accountable to me, and me only. You'll also forget the Teague woman. You ain't got the right to make aspersions, Pike . . . not any more. As for the Macaw business . . . I've somethin' else in mind.'

For the first time, Huck offered his thoughts. 'I agree with you, Pa. Amelia Teague's sort of OK . . . pretty too. She . . .'

Genner looked enquiringly at his son. 'What do you know of Miss Amelia Teague?' he asked.

'We've met.'

'When?'

'This morning at the hotel, She had nowhere . . . no one to look after the little boy while she attended the inquest. I was in the hall and said I'd help. It's as simple as that.'

'Help look after a toddler? He ain't much smaller'n you, Huck.' Genner was surprised.

'There was a girl works in the hotel. She helped.'

'What did you do?' Genner asked, curiously interested.

Huck flashed a short impertinent look at his father. 'I helped *her*. At the time it was the best option available.'

Genner went quiet for a second, then chuckled. 'Your ma wanted you brought up bell, book an' candle, Huck. She'd be pleased I reckon,' he said thoughtfully. 'Nevertheless, you stay a jump from this girl until we learn more about her an' the kid.'

Branca grunted. 'What more you want to know? Comin' from somewhere where no one knows her. She buys the Meadow, blind. Where'd she get the money? If she's the kid's aunt, where's his ma an' pa?'

Genner's voice betrayed its exasperation: 'Where was yours, Pike? Perhaps it don't pay to know everythin', eh?'

'She's just got here,' Huck joined in. 'What would you want from her, Pike . . . a public meetin' from atop the stage? "Dear Fishtail. If you don't like the look of me and my two-year-old sidekick . . . well, I'll climb right down and we'll head straight back to Butte".'

Genner relaxed, even grinned a little as Huck went on:

'Perhaps she could have turned the weener into a sandwich man . . . made him walk up and down the street. Not that it would have helped any,' he added scornfully. 'There's hardly anyone in Fishtail can read.'

Branca banged one fist into another. 'We're meant to be keepin' a hold on this valley. That's what I'm paid for, an' I'll do it any way I please.'

As if in ritual contest, Genner placed his own huge hands flat on his desk. 'I'm beginnin' to think you've been doin' that for too long, Pike. With all the time you're spendin' in town lately, who's been runnin' my ranch? You leavin' it all to Furloe Stilt?'

'I make him earn his money. As for tendin' to ranch business . . . I'm on my way there right now.'

Genner picked up Macaw's old pistol, dragged at the corroded mechanism. 'At this time of the evenin' you're ridin' back to the ranch . . . an' in that condition?' he stated incredulously. 'If I was you, Pike, I'd keep your dust right here in town. Get yourself roostered at the Bear Pit.'

'Why would I want to do that?'

'Because tomorrow you're goin' up to Big Soak. You're gonna relieve Gibson.'

Branca's expression turned hostile. Big Soak was a lake near the end of the tree-line, forty miles nearer the mountains. It was summer pasture for the vast JUG herd. 'Why?' he demanded.

'I'm gonna sound out a few o' these newcomers,' Genner said. 'There's some, includin' the Teague woman, who's maybe gonna have to move on . . . an' I don't need your sort o' help.'

'What the hell's come over you all of a sudden?' Branca raged. 'You seen the light or somethin'? This is more'n managin' the valley.' The foreman was shaking, sensed his imminent downfall. 'You aimin' to clean out all the rat-runs as well?' he sneered. 'Whatever she's done, this Teague girl's no worse than some I've known. You and me both.'

At Branca's insinuation, Huck snatched at his hat and stomped from the office.

Genner and his foreman stared at the door as it banged shut, then at each other.

'That's another reason, Pike. I'm tired of your mouth, as well as your doin's.' Genner's temper had darkened and the atmosphere in the small office was extreme. Branca knew then, there wasn't much chance of a put-back.

'You'll go to the lake, or it'll be Billings for the murder of Smiles Macaw. Make your choice.'

The rawness of Branca's features worsened. He felt the fear and uncertainty of already having pushed Genner too far. The rancher would make no compromise. It was hands-up time for Branca and both men knew it.

For a minute, Branca considered his prospects in the longer term; life without the support and benefits of JUG. 'It's your play, Boss,' he came up with as he turned to the door.

'It always is, Pike. You just forgot for a while,' Genner coldly reminded him.

8

Gather at Woodside

Rio Sand was caring and friendly, but when stressed or pushed, his temperament wasn't too accommodating. He was deeply loyal, and a strike at someone close was also a strike at him. His pulse rate increased when he thought of the rifleman firing down on his brother; when he thought of the set-up behind such a treacherous act.

It crossed Rio's mind that the timber-line of Elk Valley was ideally suited to a bushwhacker. Whoever had fired at Lenny might still be hidden in the trees, maybe even waiting to develop his gutless piece of work. Rio realized he was an inviting figure against the cobalt skyline.

But as he rode higher along the narrow trail, he became more relaxed. Behind and below him, a watery ribbon of Plum Creek rippled shiny silver. That was when the horse lowered its head to the water and sneezed at the sudden chill, momentarily lost its footing in the bankside shale. Rio tensed and reined back, but his reaction was too late. The horse reared and lunged, its front hoofs pawing at the water's edge. Then it turned and bolted and Rio fell.

As he tumbled from the saddle he groped wildly. But he'd almost done a complete somersault when he landed – crashing through roots that had grown tangled between rocks and mossy crevices.

He felt the smack of cold, and knew he'd hit the surface of the creek. He went under, then fought his way to the surface. The water was stimulating but he'd hit his head and his senses were blurred. Struggling against the pain, he overarmed towards the spiky outline of trees along the shore. As he felt the rock-jumbled bottom of the pool under his boots, he straightened up. He groped until his fingers clawed around the overhanging branch of a fallen pine.

He steadied himself, gasping for more air, then pulled himself up on to the bank of the creek. Exhausted, he stretched for a moment, sodden and chilled to the bone.

He thought he heard a noise, relaxed himself, trying to stop his teeth chattering. He waited, wondering where his horse was and the scatter-gun. When he heard the crack of twigs he knew it was close – real close. He pushed himself woozily to his feet, fingering the water-thinned blood that ran down the side of his face.

The boy was standing twenty feet away. He was holding the reins of his own mount and Rio's young chestnut mare.

'What happened? I'm Huck Genner,' the boy said, civilly; not in the manner that implied Rio, or anyone else should have known who he was.

'I fell in. How about you, Huck Genner?'

'I'm taking the trail between Fishtail and the JUG. There's no claim on this strip of land, is there?'

'No there isn't. Just that it's normally only used between Woodside an' Meadow Ranch. Wander off the trail down on the eastern marshes, an' you're in big trouble . . . with them rattlers an' the like.'

'Yes I know that. I also know this part of the trail can be rode as a short cut between Fishtail and the JUG.' Huck Genner suddenly looked worried. 'Who are you?' he asked. This time his manner implied that he'd already guessed the answer.

'The workin' half a' Woodside . . . Rio Sand.' Rio looked interestedly at the mount Huck Genner had been riding. 'I still don't savvy you takin' this trail. The wagon road's longer, but a powerful more easy on the hoof.'

'Not this time. The horse went lame a few miles out of town. Perhaps I should have gone back.'

Rio stepped forward, bent to pick up his hat. 'Yeah,' he said, 'maybe you should. There's still another seven or eight miles to the JUG . . . to your ranch. If you were ridin' alone, you didn't say whether you saw or heard anyone else hereabouts.'

'I haven't seen or heard anything, except the noise of your plunge. Why'd you ask?'

'It don't matter none,' Rio said, believing the boy. 'You can take my horse,' he added, out of the blue. 'I can't let *you* go it alone on foot, but *I* can.'

Huck Genner nodded, smiled. 'I was told you and your brother were pretty wild. Seems that could have been a flawed reckoning.'

'Or a prejudiced one. You've met my brother?'

'Yeah. I've also been told he owns a moro stallion. I'd like to see it one day.'

'Yeah, sure, as long as you don't make him an offer for it.'

Rio didn't look to see if his remark was having an effect. Instead, he said that he'd be needing his scatter-gun. 'You armed Huck? Don't want to frighten you none, but . . .' he started to say, as he pulled the big gun from its scabbard.

'Yeah, I know,' Huck said. 'There's booger-men loose in these hills.' He grinned openly. 'Thanks, Mr Sand . . . Rio, but the loan of your horse is all I'll need to see me home.'

Rio returned the grin. 'I don't doubt it. What about your own mare?'

'She'll follow on . . . won't be any trouble. How about you? Where'll you be?'

Rio looked himself up and down. 'At the Meadow ranch, I guess. I know it don't seem likely, but that's where the trouble's likely to start.'

It wasn't what Huck was expecting, and as he rode towards JUG he thought long about Rio's stirring and enigmatic response.

There was no one about when Furloe Stilt approached the yard that fronted the Woodside cabin. He rode around to the rear and dismounted, loose-tied his horse by the small corral, noticed the moro. Then warily he walked to the nearest window, looked through at the food store and plain kitchen.

He turned to the side of the cabin, carefully moved aside a slatted shutter from the next window. The room was bigger, clean and simply furnished. There was a cowhide stretched across one wall and a buffalo skin on the foor. On a low table he could see a black bag; beside it some small bottles, a wad of cotton and an open book. A cot had been pushed into one corner, and on it lay Lenny Sand. His eyes were closed, and except for his boots he was still fully dressed. He'd been bandaged around his midriff and his left hand was wrapped tightly in bloodied cotton strips. He appeared to be in a deep sleep.

'Hit him twice. Two out of three ain't so bad,' thought Stilt. He turned away, stared into the distance. North from where he stood, was Meadow Ranch. That would be it, he realized. No one had ridden south, that was JUG land. The brother, Rio Sand, had gone after the Teague girl.

Stilt allowed himself a cunning grin. He'd have the time he needed now.

He quickly went back to the corral where Lenny Sand's stallion was snatching at grass with a few other horses. The moro lifted his head suspiciously as Stilt got close, but the JUG man was good with livestock. The stallion was generally suspicious of strangers, but offered little resistance to Stilt's animal wisdom. It bared his teeth and gave an exploratory kick, but quickly allowed itself to be separated from the others and hitched outside the corral.

Instinct and the gentle clink of spurs aroused Lenny from his delirium, his pain-induced slumber. 'That you Ed? Rio?' he called weakly; his words failing as he saw Furloe Stilt staring down at him.

'Been offerin' yourself up for a turkey-shoot?' Stilt asked offensively.

Through watery eyes, Lenny placed Stilt; Pike Branca's top hand. 'You should know,' he said.

'Got me pegged wrong, Sand. If you been in a fight, it ain't nothin' to do with me,' he lied. 'I just got here . . . came on business for Pike Branca.'

'I've taken care of any business I had with him. What do you want?' Lenny asked croakily.

'He sent me to settle up on the moro. I ain't surprised . . . always knew he'd got a thing about that stallion o' yours.' Stilt fished around in one of his pockets and pulled a roll of notes, tossed them on to Lenny's cot. 'Two hundred dollars,' he explained.

Lenny was stretching his good hand away from the cot, down to the floor and his Colt .44. He moved a bit, blinked back some clarity, swore viciously.

'Someone like Branca makes you wonder how such a life form stays alive. Must be somethin' real primitive, I guess.' He looked sadly at Stilt. 'He knows the horse ain't for sale, an' you're a liar. Take the money and get out.'

It was plain on Stilt's face that he had no real side for the argument. He'd already considered shooting Lenny – finishing him off. But up close and personal was different from the work of a rifleman.

'I was sent to fetch the moro,' he insisted.

If only Stilt had known of Branca's fall from grace with Genner, he wouldn't have been so stubborn about it. He might have ridden away there and then.

Lenny tried to manoeuvre himself nearer to the edge of the cot, get his hand nearer the Colt.

Stilt stood watching, uncertain. When it came to taking the moro by force there was Genner to think about as well as Branca. It was the same as horse stealing. The small ranchers were repeatedly obliged to sell Genner a piece of land, a horse or a good bull at *his* price. But to simply take a thing because he'd enough might to do it, went against his unique law.

The way it was stacked up, it was necessary that Stilt rode the trail between Branca and Genner; satisfy one without crossing the other. He took a pencil stub from his waistcoat pocket.

'I've had an idea,' he said, looking around the room

for something to write on. 'You're gonna write me out a ticket for the stallion.'

Lenny groaned. The Sand brothers were involved in more than a struggle for the possession of a horse. Nevertheless, he wasn't going to let Stilt take the moro. He had to make a move for his gun.

The creaking of the cot warned Stilt, who'd just finished scribbling some figures on a scrap of paper. He whirled, but although he immediately understood Lenny's intent, he wasn't quick enough and his hands were full.

Lenny had rolled from the cot, got to half standing. The room spun around him madly. He felt as though he was coming apart; his legs sinking in a deep oozy bog, his head and shoulders floating towards the ceiling. He couldn't make it to his gun and he backed against the logged wall for support.

In one movement, Stilt dropped the pencil and paper, dragged his Colt from its holster. He had no time to lift the barrel and fire though, as Lenny's right hand caught him in the middle of his forehead. Lenny had managed to grip hold of a heavy basin and it split Stilt's skin. He saw blood spurt, before he made another despairing grab for the Colt.

But he'd used up his will-power and remaining strength. Stilt's heavy gun came up and, unable to react, Lenny felt it pound into his jaw. With his left hand clutched painful and useless across his chest, he went heavily back to the floor.

He landed on his wounded side, the agony sending an unbearable wave through his body. He drew in his knees, made a useless sideways move to rise again. Stilt lashed out with his boot, which caught him hard in the shoulder.

Stilt wiped a thick smudge of blood across his face, kneeled to pick up the piece of paper. 'You'll put your name to this,' he snarled at Lenny, 'or I'll put one more bullet into you.' The man pointed the barrel of his Colt between Lenny's eyes.

Lenny's tortured mind held on. If Furloe Stilt had been a cold-blooded killer, he'd be dead already. Lenny could almost smell the man's fear. He knew Stilt wasn't far off pulling the trigger, but it would be out of anger and frustration. He thought he'd find out – one way or the other.

'I'll see you in hell, mister,' he said with his fading senses.

As his eyes closed, he saw a finger crush the trigger of the Colt. Lenny awaited the red flames but nothing happened outside of his own darkness. Instead, Stilt dropped the Colt and stumbled backwards.

Neither man had heard the riders. Three people stood in the doorway that adjoined the small kitchen. Amy Teague was holding Dub in tight, Rio Sand was levelling the scatter-gun.

Slipping in and out of consciousness, Lenny attempted a weak, thankful grin.

Amy looked from Lenny to Stilt who was crowded up against the wall, then at Rio. Dub did the same, then looked up at her.

'You've just about met all our neighbours now. You're going to like it here Dub, I just know it,' Amy said.

Rio and Amy stepped over to Lenny.

'It was Amy,' Rio said softly. 'She said we should ride back over the ridge instead of going round it. Just as well, eh brother?' He watched Amy peel away a thick dressing from Lenny's side; saw the blood welling again. He swallowed emotionally, indicated for Amy to avert

Dub's attention. He stepped in close to Stilt and swung the butt of the scatter-gun low into the man's stomach. 'Bet someone told you I was the buck nun,' he murmured. Then as Stilt crumpled, he slashed the barrel against his jaw and mouth.

He carried his brother back to his cot, gritted his teeth at the colourless features and beaded sweat.

'What's gonna happen to my hand, Rio? Tell me the truth . . . you must o' seen it,' Lenny asked, quiet and resigned.

'Do you remember Pa readin' to us about someone who said, "one hand's as good as two, if you know how to use it"? Do you remember that, Lenny?'

Lenny squeezed his eyes shut against the pain. 'That was a dime-store novel . . . weren't real,' he murmured.

Amy helped, and as they laid him down, Rio noticed the roll of banknotes. He thought for a second, then went to pick up Stilt's slip of paper. When he'd read the few words, his face darkened.

'So Lenny was gonna sell the moro for two hundred dollars was he? No need to question our friend here who's behind all this then,' he added.

Rio screwed up the piece of paper and stuffed the dollars into Stilt's pocket. Without saying a word to Amy he dragged Stilt into the yard; let him collapse into the dust while he went to find his horse.

As Dub watched from the front doorway, Rio pig-stringed Pike Branca's top hand across the saddle of his horse. He took a long look at his handiwork, then stepped back into the cabin. For the first time he noticed the cloying cut of salts and iodine spirit that emanated from his brother's bloody wounds.

'Lenny needs a doctor, Rio. He's hurt bad,' was Amy's worried greeting.

Rio nodded. 'Yeah, I know. I wish I knew what happened to Edwards. He musta gone for somethin'.'

Amy shook her head. 'No. I mean proper doctoring, Rio.'

Rio looked hard at the girl. 'You up to ridin' into Fishtail?' he asked. 'Ain't no place for a lady after dark.'

'Then I'll take this.' Amy held up Lenny's Colt .44. 'I'm more worried about Dub. You Sands seem to attract trouble.' There was no humour in Amy's response.

'He'll be all right here. Just supposin' the sawbones refuses to come?'

Amy's eyes flashed. 'He'll come.' The smile left Rio in no doubt of her ability to return with Doctor Chillum.

'Take the moro,' he said. 'If there *is* any trouble, you'll be able to outrun it.'

9

The Doctor's Game

Its ears pricked forward, the stallion trotted watchfully down the deserted main street of Fishtail. As they passed the most recent of the town's blood-bucket saloons, Amy heard the clamour of raised voices and bawdy laughter. Further along the boardwalk past the hardware store and to her left, she heard the sudden splatter of feet. Two slight figures emerged from the shadows. Both appeared to be bedraggled and bare-foot.

They leaped into the street, shouting and waving their arms. The moro snorted and shied away from the riotous behaviour. As Amy strove to calm the horse a rectangle of yellow light suddenly lit the ground and a woman stepped from an open door into a side alley.

'Beaker, Cush . . . get in here. What you doin' out there, hellin' around?'

The young troublemakers turned, tried to slope into the shadows, but the woman was up to it and grabbed at them roughly.

Amy blinked at the plain language of exasperation and upbraid, made soothing noises at the moro, as the woman shoved the boys through the door.

'The scarin' o' people's horses. The very idea. You're both on your father's road all right,' the woman cackled.

She looked up at Amy, who was holding the stallion to an irritable stomp. But as soon as she saw it was Amelia Teague, the woman's tirade against her young brood was immediately forgotten.

Despite the darkness and crispness of night, Amy felt the effective reach of Allie Macaw's vilifying. It drifted with her to a single-storey clapboarded house set back from the main street. There was an unlit lamp over the door, but Amy could read the painted shingle. A.B. CHILLUM MD. The house appeared to be empty, but she dismounted and tried the door anyway. It was locked, and her knocking aroused no reply.

Uncertain about what to do next, Amy stared into the night. Under a store lamp on the opposite side of the street, she saw the woman coming towards her. The two boys were on her own side, and Amy gripped the reins of the moro.

'I think this is the farewell party approaching. They're probably bringing an ultimatum,' Amy said, quietly taking the reins in her hand.

The two boys were ahead of the woman, their thin bodies twisting and sidling as they came on. They sprang from the boardwalk into the street, pulled faces, windmilled their arms, stamped their feet. It reminded Amy of an aged mind-blown idiot she'd once seen dancing with a bear along a quay in San Francisco.

The taller of the two boys threw a stone that arced up on to the roof of the doctor's house. Then he threw another that struck the shingle. The stone clattered off on to the boardwalk and Amy clasped her hand around the moro's nose.

'You've seen worse than this,' she murmured. 'Anyway, it's me they're trying to scare off, not you.'

The smaller boy tossed a clod that landed almost under the belly of the stallion. It tossed its head nervously and looked over its muscled shoulder.

'We haven't been hit yet,' Amy said more firmly.

Then a stone landed on the boardwalk and she heard the woman's malicious, sinister giggling.

Amy swore to herself. '*You're* who the boys get it from,' she shouted. 'Not the poor father . . . whoever he is.'

When stones struck her leg and her arm, she held the reins across the stallion's neck, grabbed the pommel and swung upward – just as a stone struck his forehead. He lunged, but Amy controlled him and turned him around, nudged him with her heels. Ears laid back and snorting, the moro launched himself across the street. In a few great pounding strides, his hoofs bore down on the young hellions.

The woman screamed a warning. Shrieking with terror all three fled, while only paces behind them the moro pummelled to a halt. The stone-throwers had jumped for the shelter of their mother and the board-walk; too close to be run down or struck by the stallion, had that been Amy's intention. She'd just sent them scuttling to cover like the wildlife they imitated.

She took a few deep breaths and walked the horse steadily until they chanced on Barney's Beers. She got in close before dismounting at some low steps; then with a sniff and a glower of anger, she crossed the boardwalk. Without stopping she pushed open the doors, and took one pace inside.

Lighted by oil-lamps that hung from low rafters, the interior was gloomy and daunting. There was one man at the bar, crowding a glass of beer. The bartender was running a sopping rag along the counter-top, and he paused to stare open-mouthed at Amy.

Amy didn't move any closer – there was no need. She smiled pleasantly.

'Can you tell me where I can find Doctor Chillum?' she asked, waiting for the drinking man to turn around.

Amy took a step closer to the bar. Take a good look, she thought.

'The doc? Why . . . err . . .' The bartender wiped his fingers in the dirty cloth. 'I don't rightly know, Ma'am. There's maybe a game at the Bear Pit. You might find him there. Enjoys his cards, does Doc Chillum. Yessir . . . Ma'am.'

'Thank you. What does he look like . . . the doctor?'

A little later than Amy had predicted, the man drinking beer turned to gape, as the bartender answered her.

'He's kinda middlin',' came the slow answer. 'Kinda faded . . . bit like a doctor, I suppose. Wears a fancy neckcloth . . . one a' them little sling hats.'

Amy nodded, gave her thanks and immediately walked out. She led the moro further down the street, crossed to the saloon. The Bear Pit was Fishtail's most established hostelry, its busiest and certainly its roughest and toughest.

From inside came some hurdy-gurdy music she'd heard earlier accompanied by loud voices and the chink of glass.

Amy gritted her teeth and went in. For a moment her nerve almost cracked, for it looked like every other man in Elk Valley had chosen that night to visit the bar. Girls in colourful, showy costumes were trading off full tables.

At the back of the bar, she saw a ring of men, two, three deep. There were one or two stretching to see over the shoulders of those in front. That would be the men "enjoying their game", Amy bet. She stepped forward, avoiding eye contact as her presence quickly became noticed.

Perhaps she could reach Doctor Chillum, make the purpose of her visit known before having to respond to unwanted attention, ward off a drunken brain.

But there were too many closely packed tables, too many customers to negotiate. She thought she'd found a pathway, moved swiftly, sensing every pair of eyes but those of the card players roving around her.

A man pushed himself to his feet, a stupid, eager grin across his thin face. Immediately, Amy plotted a new course to avoid him. But she was cut off by a run of tables which had been shoved together. On the other side, there was a bunch of men who'd backed off the bar to watch her progress.

She wasn't going back, so she went on. *Surprise 'em. Go in hard and fast.* For a fraction of a second she recalled the old army manual of her father where she'd read something similar. Stupid cliché, she said to herself, trying to block out the advancing man. *Surprise 'em.* She wondered about it, as the man's hand made a clumsy grab at her.

She turned to face him directly. 'Is Doctor Chillum one of those men?' she asked, nodding at the group of card-players. 'It's very important that I get to speak to him.'

The man withdrew his grin and his hand. He squinted, slanted his head sideways on. He was confused before, but Amy's straight question panicked him. His tongue flicked, and his mouth opened and closed. He was testing his ability to speak. 'Yeah . . . the doc. He's there . . . somewhere,' he mumbled.

He was repeating himself as Amy slipped nimbly past him.

A few seconds later the card-players heard Amy say, 'I'd like to speak with Doctor Chillum. It's urgent, please let me through.'

Two men stood back, and a gap opened between Amy and the table. There were four men seated, and it was to the man wearing the silk neckcloth that Amy looked directly.

'What do you want in here?' the man demanded. His tone was a mixture of complaint and amazement as Amy took a step closer.

'A doctor. There's a man at the Woodside ranch who's been shot. He's hurt bad,' she said hurriedly.

The doctor blew hard. 'Woodside,' he repeated, his eyes boring into Amy. 'The Sand brothers' land. Which one's been hit? What happened to him?'

'Does that matter?' Amy countered. She hadn't faced up to the contents of the Bear Pit bar to waste time answering irrelevant questions.

The physician responded stiffly. 'It helps for a doctor to know who the patient is . . . 'specially when it's a call.'

Amy's pulse increased as she realized Chillum was going to prove difficult. 'It makes a difference to the treatment you give, does it . . . knowing that? We should be leaving,' she said, the worry obvious.

Chillum casually placed his cards face down on the table. '*We?*' he reiterated. 'I haven't said I'd go anywhere, yet.'

Despite Rio's warning, Amy hadn't considered that a qualified physician would even question the help he could give.

'Your profession's meant to *save* lives, not put them at risk,' she snapped back, her voice getting more steely. 'What sort of doctor are you?'

Amy's comprehending eyes took in the hand of cards. Then she looked him straight in the face before he said anything back. 'There's a lot of witnesses here, Doctor Chillum. If you don't come with me, I'll make such a fuss you'll find it hard to even *live* in Montana . . . let alone practise.'

Amy's threat seemed to affect everyone in the saloon. The silence was so complete that she heard someone behind her whisper hoarsely, 'What was that? What was that, she said?'

The arrogant set of Chillum disappeared. Almost furtively he glanced up at the faces looking on. One of his game-partners – a man who had the look of a sales-man – spoke up.

'When people don't want help, there comes a time when they don't get it, They just get what's comin' to 'em.'

Amy shook her head. 'I think I understand you, but it's not *them* who's doin' the askin'.' Infuriated, she whirled on Chillum. 'Is that your answer? You'd have him crawl into the brush like a dying dog,' she blazed. 'Lenny Sand was hurt bad this afternoon, shot from the trees by someone too cowardly to face him. Is that what you good people of Elk Valley give support to? Was *that* what was coming to Lenny Sand?'

Amy's eyes flicked to the other man. 'I'll remember what you said, mister. I'll pass it on to Rio Sand if his brother dies.'

The man who'd voiced the spineless opinion was just smart enough to know when not to carry on with it.

Desperate, Amy turned again to Chillum. 'Do you

want me to beg? I will, if that's what you think a life's worth.'

Now she saw conflicting emotions shade the doctor's face. But before he had a chance to respond, a body reeled heavily into Amy, She was jolted to one side, momentarily losing her balance. Then she swung about to face the man she thought she'd managed to shake off.

As her new-found world turned ugly, she closed her eyes in misery. She was being encircled, hemmed in. Then the man reached out, dragged her to him.

'Why bother with him, pretty miss, when you can have a real live one?' he babbled.

'Find a mirror,' Amy almost spat at him.

She knew she'd made a mistake as the man made a grab. As she flinched away, she blazed silent appeal to the men who'd laughed.

A few squirmed uneasily, but there was no help. Like the Sand brothers, she'd been made an exile and was about to 'get what was comin' to her'.

She leaned forward, making space. Then she moved her hand down to the deep side-pocket of her riding breeches.

To the man, Amy's body gesture suggested compliance. He guffawed crudely, dropped his head close to her neck. His breath curdled hot across her face as she swung up Lenny's .44 Colt.

It was a fast, anger-powered movement that ended against the side of the man's shabby head; the crack of bone still splitting the air as he went down. Amy lashed out, disgustedly pushed him away from her. She gave a convulsive shudder as the man folded into the floor.

Warning the others off, Amy instinctively waved the barrel of the Colt. Although she was surrounded, her retaliation seemed to have stupefied the crowd. As they stared down at the blood that was already soaking into the filthy floorboards, she pushed up against the card-table. Still clutching the Colt, she challenged Chillum.

'Time and temper's up. Are you coming with me?'

The now compliant doctor picked up his cards, put them in an inside pocket. Slowly he got to his feet. 'Hell, why not,' he relented. 'It's safer than arguin' with a big unsteady gun.'

10

Fighting Prospects

Huck Genner chose not to ride Rio Sand's mare all the way home. He thought it best not to let anyone know he'd accepted a favour from one of the Woodside men; mostly because of his father's explicit instructions not to.

When he got to within a mile north of the ranch house, he dismounted under cover of a bigtooth maple. Hidden deep in the trees he unsaddled the mare and made a long tether. Carrying only the bridle he set out to walk the rest of the way.

It would be long after dark by the time he got to the yard; most hands would be inside, relaxing for a while after their supper. He could take a horse from the corral and ride back through the trees to intercept his own horse. If he left out the Rio Sand bit, he didn't need an explanation if anyone saw him. Early tomorrow, when the coast was clear, he'd take the mare back.

To young Huck, the venture carried a trace of risk, even duplicity, but within one hour he was safely back

69

inside the ranch house. He stretched himself in a big chair facing the open fireplace. He was idling away time, flicking through the pages of a catalogue when an excited cowboy ran into the kitchen.

'Huck, you there, Huck,' he called out. 'Stilt just rode in. You should see him. Trussed up he was. Looks like he met the mountain banshee.'

The earlier excitement welled again in Huck, gripped at his stomach. Furloe Stilt was Pike Branca's top hand.

'Where is he now? What you done with him?' he asked eagerly.

'Some o' the boys are with him in the bunkhouse. We . . .'

Further stuff was lost on Huck. He was already gone from the house, half-way across the yard. He ran towards the building where a row of lighted windows glowed out at him. Heart pounding, he pushed at the half-closed door.

Inside there were two JUG men bent over a figure on one of the wallside bunks, One of them was holding a lamp.

'What happened to him, Malty?' Huck asked breathlessly.

'Been messin' with someone he shouldna. He ain't workin', but he'll live,' Malty replied dourly. The ranch hand wrung out a wet cloth.

Stilt looked bad to Huck. Most of the blood had already been washed off his face, but one eye was puffed closed, and his lips were smashed and misshapen. His nose was purple, looked as if it had been beaten into the side of his face.

'Did he tell you anything yet?' Huck then wanted to know.

Malty smiled grimly, but before he could say anything, Stilt managed to open his good eye. It stared angrily, settled on Huck, and the boy shuddered.

'You get Pike here, boy. I ain't talkin' until I see him,' Stilt hissed.

Huck stuttered, 'Wasn't he . . . wasn't he, with you?'

The beaten man's mouth hardly moved. 'Stayed in town with your pa,' he answered quietly, and didn't say any more.

There was a lot Huck wanted to know, but he didn't dare ask. Stilt had drifted back into crushed silence, but Malty said he didn't think a doctor could help much. With the sudden, new-found responsibility of boss's son, Huck said the two men ought to do their best and look after Stilt until his father returned.

Huck spent a restless night in the house. He'd got up early, and when his father and Pike Branca rode in just after daybreak, his mind was still racing with what further trouble the new day would unfold.

But he stayed back, didn't go out to greet them. His youthful curiosity was unbounded, but he couldn't show it. His father would want to know the significance of his being abroad so early, and he wouldn't have an answer. To escape, Huck folded himself up again in the armchair. He knew he couldn't be seen by anyone coming into the room or walking through behind him.

He heard his father and Branca walk to the den that led off the west wall of the house. He sat listening to the strained, unnatural silence that endured between the two men. It lasted for many minutes – until other noises and low groans gave away the arrival of Stilt.

That was James Genner's way; send for a man and just assume he'd get there. Usually they did, even brought to him dead if he ordered it. There was a muffled thud, and Huck knew the heavy, leather-covered door had been pushed to.

Muttering trivial swear-words, he walked quickly and silently to the adjoining wall. With his father's first words, Huck overcame the shame of snooping.

Genner was saying: 'If Lenny Sand packs up, I'll drag you through the marshes . . . let the snappers get at you. God help me if I don't . . . you an' Pike both. Goddam it . . . what you done's as bad as backshootin'.'

There was a couple of seconds' silence before Genner finished his haranguing of Stilt. 'That's some-thin' we ain't come to yet.'

Huck could feel his blood racing. He remembered Rio Sand's threat about dishin' out trouble; wondered if there was any connection. A lot suddenly happened in his mind's eye and he missed Still's reply. He flinched as an upstairs door banged, paid attention when his father went off again.

'There was nobody needed to tell me it was you,' Genner said harshly. 'I was sat jawin' . . . playin' check-ers with Gil Frost till late. I know Pike never left his room.'

There was another short silence, then Genner carried on: 'Even before I'd rubbed sleep outa my eyes, I was told about the girl sashayin' into the Bear Pit . . . nearly takin' Chick Gannon's head off when he tried to get frisky. All she wanted was to get Doc Chillum out to Woodside. One o' the Sands had been shot up. Fired on by a coward who hid behind a tree, was what she said.'

Huck sniffed quietly, remembered that Rio Sand had asked him if he'd seen or heard anything. Like one of his old jigsaws, the small pieces were adding up.

Genner snorted. 'When I learned you weren't in town, I sort o' put two an' two together.'

That was the cue for Branca to join in. 'That's what I've been tryin to get over,' he said. 'Sand can't be hurt bad. Yeah, Furl shot him up a bit, but it was just scary stuff. Just enough to let that stallion go. He didn't . . .'

'I shoulda known you figured in it, Pike,' Genner cut in sharply. 'Now shut it. Let the toad make up his own lies. Hell, I wish I'd been in the Bear Pit,' he added more thoughtfully. 'Sounds like the Teague girl's got more guts than any two o' you.'

Expediently, Stilt seized on Branca's lie. 'That *was* the truth of it, Mr Genner,' he insisted. 'I only aimed to groove him. If he dies, it ain't down to me. I followed him down to the cabin with Pike's money. He was there . . . live enough to have a go at me when I made him an offer for the horse. I didn't mean to get rough.'

'*You* didn't mean to get rough,' Genner roared, coughed with incredulity. 'You cretin. A pile o' hog's guts is prettier than the face you're carryin'.'

'It was the other one, done that,' was Slilt's retort. 'He'd rode off to fetch the girl from Meadow Ranch. They came back all quiet like, got the drop on me. He worked on me with a big scatter-gun. I couldn't fight back . . . tried to sweet talk 'em.'

'You're a liar, Stilt, an' I guess I'll never know the truth of what happened.'

'No stallion either. Looks like we've all taken a beatin' for very little. That's gonna have to change, an' soon.' The dissatisfaction was Branca's.

'You won't be changin' anythin', Pike, except where you get yourself buried. I already told you,' Genner barked.

'You never helped along a sale . . . somethin' you

wanted, with a bit of persuadin'?' Branca whined.

'Your mouth's wanderin' again, Pike. I told you about that as well. You just don't listen. It's the way you're goin' about things now. You're not only a liability, you're a big disappointment. Not only for me, but for young Huck. If I could be sure you only meant to hassle; that you didn't tell Stilt to put some bullets into Sand because of the beating he gave *you*.'

Huck stiffened at the mention of his name. He got ready to move off, but had to hear the rest of it.

'You *can* be sure, Boss,' Branca came back with. 'Hell, when I lock horns with Sand it's gonna be personal – just me and him. Besides, you know what Furl's like with a rifle. He could have put in killin' lead if he'd wanted to.'

The case-clock in the hall suddenly made its first chime for the hour, and Huck's heart missed a beat. Then the voices moved, changed places in the den and it was enough; his nerves were getting the better of him. Fear of being discovered listening-in on his own father had him away on his toes, straight up the staircase to the safety of his own rooms. Lying across his bed, he became mellow, curiously pleased. From what Branca and Stilt had said, Lenny Sand wasn't going to die. But it sounded as though he'd be laid up for a while.

Huck then worried about Rio's mare. Somehow, he'd have to water and feed it for as long as it took. For half an hour he speculated on outcomes. It stood to his impetuous reason that, because of what had happened, the Sand brothers wouldn't take any more harassment from JUG men. Separately they'd shown their strength and resolve, but now they'd be united. Rio Sand had said he'd make trouble. Huck's blood ran hot at the thought of a confrontation.

Whether it was taking sides, or injustice, Huck didn't know. Somehow he'd become involved, learned more than he should. He'd have to tell, ask somebody about it. He could talk to the JUG wrangler. Choptank had been his confidant and friend since he'd sat Huck on a spotted pony on his second birthday.

He'd got to get away, get a horse saddled without having to answer questions. He felt guilty about Rio's mare, but taking it back would give him the chance to talk to the Sand brothers; another bit of the jigsaw.

He heard noises from the yard below and crossed to his window. Standing to one side he looked for anyone that might delay his plan. Instead, he saw Pike Branca and his father riding out of the yard. Furloe Stilt was behind, leading two pack-mules.

Until all three men were well into the home pasture, Huck watched. He felt hurt, then anger at Pike Branca for having done such a thing. The JUG foreman – a man whom he'd once looked up to – had let him down, dealt him a crushing blow. But like his father, there remained a doubt in Huck's mind. Even taking into account the latest disclosures about Branca's character and capabilities, he wasn't yet ready to believe the man capable of committing murder.

He knew that both Branca and Stilt were being punished. The old man was sending them out to replace a couple of line men from the Big Soak. It was the usual way, but not for a foreman and his top hand. His father would remain with them for a few miles; until they'd more fully understood James Umac Genner – JUG law.

11
The Offer

Apart from a few days of delirium and pain, a week's recuperation passed uneventfully for Lenny Sand. He worried about being laid up, about not being able to offer even a token resistance. He was also bothered by the knowing that as soon as he got to his feet without falling down, Rio would have him out working on the ranch.

After cleaning and rebandaging Lenny's wounds, Doc Chillum had offhandedly left behind a bottle of laudanum. Edwards had eventually returned and made up poultices of balsam and Solomon's seal. He applied them liberally to Lenny's broken hand and started some painful rehabilitation. Lenny knew it would never be good again, but was confident of getting some measure of feeling and movement back. On his own during the day, he spent hours gripping and flexing his fingers against the stiff, knotted flesh. Amy Teague cut and stitched him a tight-fitting glove out of the skin of a deer she'd shot along Plum Creek.

However it was something else that disturbed Lenny. As soon as he got his health back, Amy would return to

Meadow Ranch. He knew that as long as she stayed to administer the appropriate comforts no harm could come to her. But that was while she was at Woodside. Though him and Rio might beat a trail through the tree-line, there was no way of knowing what would happen on her own land.

Amy had grit, and she was more than proficient with a rifle. But Lenny suffered at the thought of her and Dub being alone and vulnerable. There was usually a way around a gun, and someone like James Genner was old and clever enough to know it.

Lenny couldn't ask her to spend more time at his side. Even if he over-played the poorness of his health and she agreed, it wouldn't improve the young woman's already tainted reputation. Not that he fretted over the injustice of that, but there were others to consider.

For a short, appealing while he thought about asking for her hand. But although Lenny was of the live-and-let-live breed, at that time Amy was still an enigma.

It was nothing that came from what she did or said; she was amiable and kind. It was in what she didn't say. Since telling Lenny about her sister – when he'd taken her to Meadow Ranch in his wagon – she'd not told him any more about her upbringing or family; places she'd been other than San Francisco.

Lenny's feelings were such that, being uncertain of her response, he didn't want to ask any direct questions. If that was the way she wanted it, any confidential stuff would remain her own. But it would stop him from getting involved.

Lenny's deliberations for his immediate future were put aside when, late one day, his brother returned excited from Fishtail.

'Genner's sent Branca and his top hand up to Big Soak. He must o' banished 'em . . . why else?' Rio shouted. He was still astride his chestnut mare outside the front door of the cabin.

'When was this . . . how'd you know?' Lenny asked, stepping out on to the stoop.

'Ben Chawkin told me. He wasn't sure . . . musta been more'n a week ago. Just after someone shot you up, I'm thinkin'.'

'Yeah, maybe,' Lenny agreed. 'That would account for the quiet around here. What else you thinkin'?' he asked.

'If I was James Genner, I'd want to keep things plugged in Elk Valley. Particularly after the Smiles Macaw shootin'. If the sheriff of Billings gets wind o' this, he might . . . just might decide to ride up an' have a look for hisself.'

Lenny nodded as his brother dismounted. He looked up, saw Amy walking through the meadow with Dub. 'You're right, Rio. Genner's still a sharp stick. It would be the end of his honorary rule hereabouts.'

Rio followed his brother's gaze, saw Amy swinging the kid over the pole gate into the yard. 'He'd a' known we weren't up to much, with you bein' so busted up,' he said. 'He coulda taken the opportunity to put both of us into the ground.'

'If it had just been us, yeah you're right, Rio. But you've forgot Amy . . . he hasn't. He's held back because he don't want a woman with a kid mixed up in this fight . . . whatever it's about. It's too messy. How'd you explain it to Sheriff Gane?' Lenny raised his right hand at Amy and Dub. 'No, Rio. The way I see it, he'll drive out Amy first, then it'll be our turn.'

Rio spoke quickly as Amy approached. 'Maybe that'll

divide Genner and Pike Branca. Ben Chawkin told me Branca's sweet on Amy.'

'I guessed that,' Lenny said, with a wry smile. 'But if he's goin' to cross Genner, he'd best remember exactly who it is moves cattle on the JUG range . . . who still carries the artillery.'

Lenny was right in his reckoning. Within two days, Amy Teague and the Meadow ranch got a visitor.

For nearly ten days Amy's vegetable patches had been untended. Corn, pole-beans and lettuce, were parched and limp. But it was a fine day and Amy wasn't in the tending or nursing frame of mind. With Dub beside her, she ran the buckboard out to the edge of her home pasture. She carried a bag of staples, gloves and a claw hammer, all she needed for some fence-patching. She tied the scabbard of her rifle across the rear of the seat. Lenny had advised her not to go anywhere unarmed. At that time in Elk Valley, and with her experience of the Bear Pit saloon, he'd be right.

Long continuous runs of the pasture-fence were secure, only required minor running repairs. But in the south-eastern crook she discovered a big break in the wire. The way Amy set to work it was obvious she had spent time working a ranch, not simply making sumacs or quilting on the stoop.

She was pulling on the top wire, hammering in a staple when she saw the rig approaching from the south.

The wagon road that ran most way along the valley wasn't visible from where Amy was working, so whoever it was hadn't turned off for a casual word. There must have been a purpose; that was the route from JUG, past Woodside to the Meadow, From a distance whoever it was looked big, was wearing dark clothes, and Amy guessed his identity.

She walked a few paces to the buckboard, untied and withdrew the Winchester. Dub was between the wheels playing whack a bullfrog. She took the gun back to where she was working and propped it against the inside of a post.

Not concentrating on the task, she banged in a crooked staple. She was trying to appear confident, unconcerned, but her feelings paled when she saw that it *was* James Genner.

As he rode up she straightened. She dropped the hammer and took off her gloves, rubbed her wet palms against the buckskin, pushed back her hat.

Genner slowly appraised her from head to foot; he was looking for defiance, the bravery he'd heard about.

'I've come to offer ... make a deal,' he said brusquely, almost self-consciously.

'Don't let me stop you. Go ahead, Mr Genner, make your offer.' Amy met the man's piercing grey eyes without a tremor. 'How did you know I was here ... back home?' she asked.

Genner smiled coolly. 'I know who's movin' around in my valley.'

Amy was outraged at the thought she might have been dogged, that Genner might actually believe the valley was his own. '*Your* valley,' she said with a mocking edge. 'You've men out watching over me? I really don't know that I appreciate that.'

Genner heard the sudden scorn in the girl's voice. 'A man in my position has to keep tabs on his own family sometimes,' he said, adding, 'and those who work for me, of course.' He caught the flicker of irritation in Amy's eyes.

'Of course,' she agreed.

Genner looked at Dub. 'My boy made a visit to Woodside,' he said, thoughtfully. 'That's what I came to see you about. I want you to stay clear of Huck and my foreman.'

Amy shook her head, laughed quietly. 'There's an asylum in Oakland, California. It's full of people just like you, Mr Genner.' She stared hard at the ground, thinking of what to say next. 'From what I know of him, Huck's a nice lad, but a lad, a yearling. As for Pike Branca, I think he needs roping in.'

'Pike's a grown man ... can be mule-headed,' replied Genner.

'He's mean-headed, and being of an age doesn't mean to say you're a man.'

Genner wound the reins around his huge fingers. 'I'll give you fifteen hundred dollars for this place. That's kit an' caboodle,' he said sharply.

Amy shook her head. 'If that's what you really came here for, there's no need to waste any more of your time, Mr Genner.'

'That's more than I offered Jed Tibble.'

'And less than I paid him,' Amy retorted. 'But that's not what it's about. If you doubled ... trebled it, my answer would still be no.'

Amy saw Genner's jaw twitch, his face darken. She moved her hand to the tip of the rifle barrel.

'What do you want ... how much?' he demanded impatiently.

Amy took a deep breath, remained calm. 'How much doesn't come into my reckoning. What I want is to be left alone,' she said quietly, tolerantly.

'Fifteen hundred, and five hundred more if you leave the valley. Settle somewhere Pike don't know about.'

Amy's tolerance of Genner's arrogance gave way. 'What is it with you? For heaven's sake, I hardly know Pike Branca. What I do know of him sickens me. What gives you the right to . . . what are you talking about?'

'He's gone bad since you came to Fishtail. Whichever way you cut it, lady, you've got under his skin. There's not many can say that.'

'That's his problem, Mr Genner, and you know it.' Amy pulled up the rifle, held it at her side. 'I . . . we like it here. We'd like it a lot more if people like you left us alone. I'm not moving off the Meadow. Not for you or anyone else.'

Genner said bleakly, 'You will lady . . . an' there's no need for that Winchester, I've finished here. Just remember – setting your hook in Pike'll get you nothin'. I can send him on his way with nothing more than his johns.'

'You're close to raving, Mr Genner. Get yourself to that place in Oakland while you're still able.' Amy walked to the buckboard, smiled warmly at Dub.

As Genner swung his rig around, she wondered about relationships at the JUG. Impatient for Huck to grow, perhaps Genner saw in Pike more than he should. Like a lot of power-crazy people he wanted more . . . always more. At best he was headed for a big let-down.

Amy dropped the rifle and lifted Dub on to the buckboard, heard Genner's ranting.

'Could be that talk in town's close to the truth. You won't get what you're after. Pike's gonna cool down. When he does, he'll see what species you belong to.'

As she flicked the reins, Amy wondered what could have happened to *Mrs* Genner. She held up for a second, took a last look at the rancher.

'Next time I won't hold him back,' he warned.

The look in his eyes drilled into Amy. She moved the buckboard on, thought she had the answer to Mrs Genner.

Genner spoke calmly to his black mare, walked it on.

To Amy, the deliberation and control were more worrying than an angry gallop. She shivered. The man was suffering from paranoia, obviously breaking up. Forlornly, Amy hoped he'd not remember any of it the following day.

12

Back From Big Soak

Genner had told Pike Branca to stay up at Big Soak for a month. But, feeling resentful and hard done by, he stayed less than two weeks. His battered face had begun to heal, the bruises, cracked mouth and swollen eye were getting back to normal. Only the damage left inside him by Lenny Sand was hurting; that and the humiliation of seeing the harm meted out to Furloe Stilt. But some of his old natural arrogance was returning, and above all, the isolation of not knowing was wearing away at him.

Amy Teague began to obsess him. He grew nervous of how James Genner might be dealing with her. He wanted to get back to Fishtail, somehow make amends. Any other time, he'd be confident of Genner's oiling the waters; ensuring that there'd be nobody out to rival him for a girl's attentions.

That got Branca to thinking of Lenny Sand, and his pulse raced. He thought about the night just outside Fishtail when he'd tried to buy the gleaming moro. The fight in Twine's livery stable made it twice he'd lost out.

Like the Macaw shambles, Amy Teague's presence was significant. Big Soak was too far away to know the fervour of Lenny Sand's mating dance. How deep and cosy the nest would be. And there'd be no competition to slow him down.

Night and day the contenders for Branca's fearful attention passed back and forth. Amelia Teague, Lenny Sand, the big stallion. It went on until Branca could cope with it no longer. He had to know what was going on, even though it meant taking on James Genner's temper.

Furloe Stilt, however, didn't share or appreciate Branca's decision. He too had recovered, although his face would bear lifelong scars and he'd got damage low in his belly.

It was early evening, bass were greedily taking stoneflies in the warm shallows of Big Soak. The two men were in their saddles while the horses nibbled at the lush grass. Stilt was making a cigarette when Branca announced his decision to return home.

Stilt complained immediately. 'You crazy, Pike? The old man'll torch us. He said a month. He didn't mean ten days or whatever.'

'I'll sort him out, you stay here,' Branca snapped back. 'Play with the grizzlies an' the wolves.'

Nearly two days later both men reined in their horses. They stood under cover of the maple and pine that stretched from the lake to within a mile of the JUG ranch house.

It was a view that always pleased Pike Branca. But now it brought no such feeling. 'I wonder if he's around?' he grunted. Then he nudged his horse towards the yard.

The men were just turning their horses into the corral when Huck came running from the house. He stopped short when he saw them, waited for Branca as he started towards the house.

'You're back, Pike. I thought Pa said . . .' Huck started to say, then looked worried.

Branca pretended not to notice. 'Got lonely, kid,' he answered. 'Hell, do I need some cleanin' up and some fresh duds.'

He walked resolutely to the house. He thought he'd get turned out, make it to town before his encounter with Genner. 'Where *is* your pa?' he asked casually.

'He had an early beakfast . . . rode out soon after.' Huck stepped up alongside Branca.

'I asked where he *was*, kid, not what time he ate,' Branca growled, his edginess just sounding through.

'He took his rig to Meadow Ranch,' Huck said cautiously. 'We heard Amy Teague went home. She . . .'

'Went home?' Branca stopped him short. 'Went home from where?'

Huck gave him a sideways look. 'From Woodside. She's been tendin' to Lenny Sand.' He didn't say any more, rolled his eyes in anticipation of Branca's response.

Within seconds the foreman fumed. 'Your pa sends me up to Big Soak, jus' so's Sand can get his feet under the table.' Then he swore loudly.

Stilt, who'd been following, got the meaning of Branca's outburst, did a quick turn in the direction of the bunkhouse.

It was different for Huck. He was a Genner, and safe from Branca's vengeance. The whole affair also held an earthy fascination for him. 'Pa says there's somethin' between 'em . . . Amy Teague an' Lenny Sand. Says you can't buy what they got. They . . .'

'Then I'll take. Take from 'em both,' Branca snarled. 'Damn Sand . . . just laying on a bed day after day. Her tendin' to him, while I been countin' cows.' He broke off to curse again. It was his way of dealing with the turmoil inside him.

'Pa says you was to blame for him sendin' you up country, Pike. Says it wouldn't have happened if you hadn't done what you did in Fishtail.'

'Your pa's sure said a heap, kid,' Branca sneered. Without another word he stomped up the broad steps and into the main house.

An hour later, although bathed and with a neat outfit, his dark mood hadn't lifted. He called for a fresh horse to be saddled up, then spurred it to the wagon road and headed for town.

Branca's theory was that to win a woman over, it was crucial to dominate her. In Fishtail, along Elk Valley, he'd found it to be a successful ploy over a number of years. But nothing had ever lasted, and none of the women were like Amy Teague. The further she got from him, the more it wrenched his gut. He kicked cruelly into the flanks of his mount, thought about his next move, swore bad things on those who got in his way.

It was late afternoon when Branca rode into Fishtail. He dismounted at a hitching rail, turned away as two people came out of the hardware store. He waited until he thought no one was looking, then stepped smartly into a side alley. He twisted the handle of a door in a low, narrow building and with another cautious glance around him, went in.

He was five or six hours earlier than might be his custom, but he couldn't wait to find out the comings and goings of the past ten days.

From nearby he could hear the woman shouting at her boys – the non-stop rebuke for their delinquent behaviour. They hollered back insolently, making such a noise that none of them heard him enter. He waited until the woman suddenly flung open the door ahead of him.

Instantly, Clover Wikkins's aggravation changed to composed approval. She saw the freshly groomed JUG foreman standing with his back to the inside of her front door.

'Lordy, Mr Pike,' she said, 'aren't you the early bird. Just look at me . . . I'm not even . . .'

'I want to talk to you . . . alone.' Branca quickly stopped her flustering.

'Why sure, Mr Pike,' she said, and ran to the rear of the building.

By the ensuing noise, Branca could tell Beaker and Cush Wikkins were being bundled on to the street for the rest of the evening.

Encouraged by a thin smile and the whiff of macassar oil, Clover told Branca everything that had happened since he'd gone to Big Soak. On the shooting of Lenny Sand, she suggested that there were some in town who thought maybe his wounds had been self-inflicted. Doc Chillum couldn't say otherwise. Maybe it was for sympathy. Or for the attention of his neighbour, Amelia Teague, Clover added riskily.

But Branca was brightening a little. Maybe Genner could be easing up a little, still supporting him as he'd done for so many years.

Then he thought of something else, ground his teeth. It was Clover's account of Amy taking on the Bear Pit saloon, single-handed. He was hurt, maddened that she'd been ready to stake so much to get help out to

Sand. In his confused mind he saw her alongside the moro stallion. Yeah, that was it, fire and brimstone. Oh yeah, he'd have them both. His blood raced at the thought of it.

He was looking straight at Clover, but he hardly saw her. 'Has she been back here ... to town ... since then?' he asked distractedly.

'No, I don't think so. I would have heard. Sand's brother, Rio, collects mail for them and the Meadow ranch, but I don't think she gets any.' Clover looked curiously at Branca. 'Funny the way she came out here, Mr Pike. With the kid ... not knowin' anybody ... nobody knowin' her.'

'Except....' Branca left off stating his obvious thought. Often he'd wondered about Amy Teague and Dub Horley, but had no intention of discussing it.

'Maybe someone'll turn up,' he said instead. 'Kith or kin to throw a line on her.' Branca gave Clover a conniving wink.

The anxious girl put her hand to a damp ringlet. 'You stayin' or comin' back later?'

As Branca stood on the step looking towards the main street, Clover moved up close behind him. 'Well?' she asked, shamelessly.

'Later. Put on somethin' pretty,' he said, hedging his bets.

While he downed his first whiskey, Branca stood alone at the bar of the Bear Pit. In a corner, there was an early poker-game, and he sauntered to the table.

'Mind if I join in?' he asked.

'Pull up a chair, Pike. We've sure missed your money, haven't we, boys?' Doc Chillum enquired light heart-edly of the two men sitting opposite him. Then he turned to the man sitting to his right. 'That all right with you, Mr Milton?'

The stranger casually tipped his hat, gave an agreeable nod.

'This is Mr Milton from Sioux Falls, Pike,' Chillum said. 'Got here on today's stage.' The doctor held out his hand at Branca and looked at Milton. 'This is Pike Branca. Foreman of the JUG ranch.' He introduced the two men.

To Branca's surprise, Milton unwound his lanky frame and stood up, held out his hand. 'Foreman of the JUG,' the man repeated. He sounded pleased. 'You'll be workin' for the man I've come to see ... James Genner?'

'Yeah, that's right.' Branca was thrown a bit, wondered what it was about, why he didn't know about someone who'd travelled nearly 700 miles.

Milton saw the look. 'My father,' he said, 'him and Mr Genner were partners, worked along them frenchy-named lakes, years ago. I've got an important letter for him ... very important.' Milton seemed unsure whether to sit down again at the table. 'When were you headin' back to the ranch?' he asked.

Branca was curious. 'We *could* leave right now,' he suggested warily.

Milton sat down and smiled tolerantly. 'Well, not *right* now,' he drawled. 'But I would like to ride with you.' He glanced at the pile of coins he'd already won. 'Can't leave while I'm bein' entertained so very open handedly. Havin' come this far, the letter'll keep another day.'

And keep it did. The game lasted until daybreak the following morning. The valley was still shrouded in its thick carpet of mist when Branca and Milton left the saloon. Branca strong-armed a horse from Esbert Twine, then called them up an early breakfast at the hotel. Shortly after they rode for the JUG.

Branca had spent the night pacing backwards and forwards between Clover Wikkins's house and the saloon. He was ill at ease, unsatisfied on all fronts. He was bothered about the man from Sioux Falls to the extent that, for once, he'd found the game of poker tedious, long drawn out. But he'd had some time to think. He could hardly wait to be alone with Milton, ask him a few questions.

But his impatience wasn't going to be tempered just yet. Branca reined in, when he was waved down by Furloe Stilt at the end of town. Branca's man was on his way to get his own early feed at the grub house. He stepped into the street, held the bridle of Branca's horse.

'In case you're wonderin', I followed you in,' he said, before Branca could ask the question. 'I weren't gonna get gulled by the old man when he turned up . . . no sir. You put yourself up for that, Pike.'

Branca swore silently to himself. He couldn't do much with Milton in tow, and he didn't want to upset Stilt. Over a period of time, they'd got too much on each other to hold more than a niggling grudge.

'Some sort of problem, gentlemen?' Milton asked, sensing difficulty.

'Nothing you'd be interested in,' Branca said quickly as he pulled his horse away.

Branca made awkward, brittle conversation on the ride out to JUG. At no time did Milton offer any more of an explanation as to his coming to Fishtail.

As soon as they rode into the ranch yard, Branca

shouted for Malty to take care of the horses. 'Where's the boss?' he asked anxiously.

'Rode out to see Birdham. He's putting winter stores into the eastern line shacks.'

Branca's pulse raced. Grange Birdham and Genner went back a long way. Until recently, Branca had been Genner's trusted and personal aide. But Birdham was an old-time confidant.

Something was about to happen, and Branca realized that if he'd stayed up at Big Soak, it would be without him. But with Genner away, at least he'd have the time and space he'd been waiting for.

He guided Milton towards the house, led him up on to the veranda. He opened the heavy solid door, indicated that Milton should enter. Milton stepped inside and Branca pushed the door to behind him.

He hooked his thumbs in his wide black gunbelt, raised his chin slightly. 'From Sioux Falls you say. And your father was a friend of Mr Genner's from the Dakotas,' he said threateningly.

Milton nodded. 'That's what I said. You got a problem with that?'

'Oh, yeah, Mr Milton, I've got a problem with it. James Genner ain't never been to Sioux Falls or the Dakotas. He came out to Elk Valley from the Goodnight–Loving trail. "Never been further east than the Missouri River an' never want to". I must have heard him say that a thousand times.' Branca unhooked his thumbs. 'Now you tell me what you're doin' here, Mr Milton, or I'll beat the pap outa you an' kick you to the creek.'

Milton stood very still, nothing flickered while he thought. 'We're all alone here?'

'The kid might come in. But I'll be tendin' to you

before he does, so tell me,' Branca rasped.

'My name *is* Milton, and it's true that I'm here to see James Genner. The rest was a bit of flim-flam for those in the card game.'

Branca sniffed. 'Go on,' he said.

'I was told by someone in Butte that James Genner was the man to see . . . the man who could help. I need to see him . . . ask some questions before folk start asking questions about *me*.' Milton eyed Branca carefully. 'I don't have to tell you any more than that.'

Branca smiled nastily. 'I already told you, Mr Milton. Huck Genner'll be here any minute, so spit it out.'

Milton looked pensive. 'Perhaps it'll make a difference . . . damp you down a bit, if I show you my badge,' he suggested.

'Badge? You're a lawman?' Milton took a step back.

'A detective. You've heard of the Western Executive Agency?'

'No.' Branca was nonplussed, getting twitchy. 'What do you want? Who are you after?' he asked, his mind suddenly racing.

Milton's voice broke up his imaginings. 'I trailed the person I'm seeking to Butte. For a while I lost them. But now I believe they're here in Elk Valley.'

Branca blew hard with anticipation. 'Give me a name . . . who is he?' he asked with growing impatience.

Milton looked thoughtfully at Branca, almost smiled. 'There's no need for you to go up against me, making threats. Why don't you help?' he proposed calmly. 'I get the feeling there's something in it for you.'

Branca's eyes narrowed. 'Who is he, goddammit? The man you've followed here.'

'The person I'm looking for is a woman, not a man. Young, fetching red-head, got a kid in tow. Her name's

Cornish. Hannah Amelia Cornish. In Monterey there's been a "wanted for murder" notice out on her for more'n a year.'

13

Something To Die For

Amy Teague rode off without the Winchester. Together with a few tools and her gloves she'd left it lying in the grass. Her mind had taken enough. After James Genner had said his piece, hammering at a stretch of damaged fencing suddenly didn't seem that important. With Dub beside her, she'd run the buckboard fast home.

It was towards evening and Amy had her eyes closed. She was gasping at the gush of cold running pump water when Rio and Lenny Sand rode in.

She heard them first, before towelling water from her eyes.

'Lenny. You shouldn't be riding so soon. Specially aboard that beast.' She held out her hand at the moro's nose, smiled warmly. 'Rio. You trying to finish him off?'

'There's work to be done, Miss. Wood choppin', raisin' the new barn, ploughin' an' the like.' Rio laughed.

Tentatively, Lenny swung one leg to the ground, slipped his other boot from the stirrup. He was stiff in the waist but had fairly good use of his arms and legs. He'd lost weight, and some of his weather-beaten colour. Amy noticed the awkward way in which he held his gloved left hand, but it was obvious he'd regained some toughness.

'Take more'n a couple o' bullets to finish me off,' he said, sensing her thoughts.

She shrugged. 'OK. You might as well put your horses into the corral. You'll both be staying for supper.'

'Both of us?' Rio said teasingly. 'Where's the button?'

'Land of dreams . . . lucky little fellow. Don't worry, we won't wake him.'

While Rio busied himself with a few weighty chores, Amy, with a little help from Lenny, managed to produce fried potatoes and corn with the stewed beef.

They were relaxed with coffee, laughing at tales of Rio's nursing, when they heard a rider approaching. It was the sound of a gallop. Lenny blew out the lamp and Rio moved a curtain aside. Remaining hidden, he peered out through a window.

The brothers had acted so quickly, Amy realized they were still wearing their guns. Their joking and chit-chat had been for her sake. Beneath that, they were both ready to beat up a storm.

'Can you see who it is, Rio?' Lenny said, calmly.

'Yeah,' Rio answered slowly. 'It's the Genner kid . . . looks like he's got my mare with him.'

The moonlit figure climbed from his saddle and hitched two horses to the corral, had a quick look at Lenny's stallion. As he approached the house, he called out. 'Amy . . . Amy Teague. It's me, Huck Genner.'

Amy stepped to the door, pulled it open. 'Huck? What's wrong?'

'Trouble, I think. Somethin' I've got to tell you. Pike Branca brought home a stranger this afternoon. He came in on yesterday's stage. He said he's. . . .'

Huck stopped at the rasp of a match. Its bright flare suddenly lit the room beyond Amy as she stood on the stoop. Lenny had relighted the lamp, and in its glow, Huck's face looked pale and nervous.

'It's all right,' said Amy. 'Come in.'

Uneasily, Huck came through the doorway. He stared first at Lenny then at Rio. It was Amy who spoke.

'This stranger who came to Fishtail came from Monterey, said he was a detective. That's right, isn't it, Huck? That's what you were going to say?' she asked quietly.

Huck stared at her, confused. 'You know? It's true . . . what he said?'

'That I'm wanted for murder?' A tiny muscle in the corner of one of Amy's pale-blue eyes twitched. 'Yes that bit's true, Huck.' She turned to Lenny. 'Now you know why I came to Elk Valley.'

From Lenny's expression, it was clear he was stunned.

Amy made it clearer. 'I shot my sister's husband,' she said.

Lenny's gaze held hers. He said simply, 'I guess he deserved it.'

Amy felt her legs buckle. But Lenny was there, supporting her to her fireside rocker. She blinked, saw Huck looking on, open-mouthed. She tried to smile some reassurance.

'It's all right, Huck,' she told him. 'I've known it was bound to come out. It still comes as a bit of a shock though.' She swallowed hard, her eyes on Lenny. She could see the questions in his face.

'Sounds like you got a story to tell, Amy,' he said.

'Yes. It's what I told you about my sister, Lenny. It was the truth. I just left out some of it.'

'Which "some of it"?' he asked.

'Freyer went to San Francisco, looking for Clark. I told you he died shortly after Dub was born, but he didn't. He abandoned Freyer and Dub . . . left them destitute.'

'Why?' Lenny asked.

'He didn't want the responsibility of a wife and child. He thought they'd tie him down. He was a footloose seaman . . . wanted the girl in every port.'

'And that's why you killed him?' Rio was incredulous.

'No, that's not the reason. That's nothing like the reason.' Amy shook her head slowly. 'When our father died it was up to me to sell the ranch. I went to the bank in Carson City. They helped me . . . took care of the sale proceeds. It was a great deal of money.' Amy saw the curiosity in Lenny's eyes. 'That's when I set out to find Freyer,' she carried on. 'She was living in Monterey. I wanted to tell her about father . . . the money.'

'Half of it was hers, wasn't it?' Huck wanted to know.

'Not for long, Huck. Freyer was already dying of typhoid fever. A doctor said it was probably caused by rat fleas . . . probably another gift from Chappey.'

'So, half the estate became the child's . . . Dub's,' Lenny said.

'No, it didn't. Dad was never going to make provision for any child of Freyer's. No, it reverted to me . . . all of it.'

'Not a lot this Chappey character could do about that, was there, Amy?' Rio threw in.

'He didn't see it that way . . . didn't know. That's why he came back. Even before I'd got Freyer's burial arranged.'

'What did he do?' Huck pressed forward as Amy's drama unfolded.

'He'd thought it out. He was always quick to know where the next dollar was coming from. He came to my hotel room.'

Lenny and Rio exchanged glances. They both knew Amy had reached the nub of her story, half guessed the outcome.

'It was about a week after Freyer's death. I was packing . . . going back to Carson City . . . not expecting a stinking, rot-gutted sailor to stagger into my room. He said, he'd come for Dub . . . that I couldn't have him. He spoke as though Dub was another bottle of whiskey.'

The two men and Huck remained silent, engrossed, and Amy continued:

'First Mate Chappey did what he was good at then . . . changing tack.' Amy joked. Her faint, caustic smile breaking into a grimace as she went on. 'I said "no", that Dub was all the family I had. Then he came at me . . . said *I* was the one he'd really wanted all along. He said Freyer had just followed him . . . said some awful things about her . . . my sister.'

'What did you do, Amy?' Huck asked eagerly.

'Shut it, Huck,' Lenny snapped.

Amy looked considerately at the Genner boy. 'Started unpacking,' she answered quietly. 'Dad had given me a gun . . . a derringer. It was to "safeguard my honour" he'd said. It was in the bag. It was so frightening . . . Dub was there. I reeled away and pulled the trigger. It was practically in his face . . . he was so close. It was all I could . . .' Amy blinked, shuddered at the horror of the memory.

'How'd you escape?' Rio asked quickly. Lenny just sat looking.

'The outside steps . . . the fire escape. I grabbed Dub and the bag and we ran. I had some money on account at the bank and went to get it . . . all that was there. We got to San Francisco and caught the train north. I stayed at Portland and Seattle for a while. Then I came east . . . took the Northern Pacific to Missoula.'

There was an uneasy silence and Amy gave Lenny a half-hearted smile. 'I stayed there a month,' she said. 'Then we moved on to Butte. I didn't know what to do . . . where to go next. I could hardly raise a smile from Dub. He needed to be with other children, I knew that. That's when I thought of giving myself up, Dub would have been all right. It isn't as though he'd always be penniless.'

'How'd you know that?' Rio asked, sounding doubtful.

'Because I've made out a trust fund. He gets it when he's older.'

'How old?' Huck wanted to know.

'Seventeen.'

'Phew,' the youngster came out with.

'It was in Butte that I heard about Elk Valley. The manager of the bank told me he knew about a small ranch for sale. It turned out to be Meadow Ranch.'

'Providence?' Lenny asked.

'It seemed like it. I was there with Dub *and* the money. Providence is what fools lay the blame on . . . so they say. No, Lenny, it was a gamble and I lost.'

'No you haven't, Amy. No more than we have. Anyone that lives under the influence of . . .' Lenny stopped, turned to Huck. 'Time you went home Huck. Our talk's likely to get a bit close to home . . . your home. Some o' this ain't for your ears.'

Huck coloured a little. 'I've heard things *in* my

home,' he said. 'That's why I came . . . to tell you . . . Amy.'

'Yeah, that's right Huck, sorry,' Rio said. 'Tell us how the detective got roped in with Branca. How'd you know it?'

'They were in the saloon . . . the Bear Pit. The detective said he'd been told in Butte that Pa could help him find the person he was after.'

'When was this?' Rio asked.

'They rode in about noon. I was in the house, reading when they came in. There's a big chair . . . you can't see anyone sitting in it. I thought it was Pike and Pa, so I just sat. They both been in a bad mood recently.' Huck looked at the faces around him for understanding. Amy smiled, nodded and he carried on talking. 'If Pike found out I was there, he'd have beat me, or somethin' worse.'

Lenny smiled reassuringly. 'He ain't gonna beat you, kid . . . or anythin' else. Tell us why this detective was talking to Branca.'

'Pike was threatening him – said he'd beat the pap out of him. He said he'd never let Milton take Miss Amy away . . . threatened to kill him if he did.'

Amy gasped, looked unbelieving at Huck 'He said what?' she cried out.

'That's what he said, ma'am. Then Milton said for Pike to help him; said that Dub's grandfather would pay well to get custody.'

'What the hell's goin' on here, Lenny . . . Amy? Somebody tell me,' Rio huffed.

'Huck?' Lenny implied that Huck should carry on.

'Pike agreed to get the boy . . . Dub. The detective'll go back to Monterey and say that Amy's dead.'

'I still don't . . .' Rio started again.

Amy finished the story. 'I'm served up for Pike Branca. It's blackmail. Branca knows I'll stay for the sake of Dub. I lose him either way.'

'Anythin' else, Huck?' Lenny asked.

'Yeah. I saw 'em in the yard. Pike harnessed up a coaster. The two of 'em loaded up boxes an' salt-sacks. Pike told some of the boys he was goin' back to Big Soak; goin' to bring back trout. But Pike ain't ever done that,' Huck sneered. 'He's just keepin' clear of Pa.'

'Is that all, Huck?' Lenny asked after a few seconds.

Huck shook his head. 'No, not all. Pike said he wanted the moro. Before he left he gave Furloe Stilt some money. Told him to stay behind and keep tabs on you an' Rio an' Amy.'

Rio laughed. 'I hope it was a bundle . . . after last time, eh, Lenny?'

'Yeah,' Lenny said, his mind on something else. 'Could Stilt have followed you here?' he asked Huck.

'No, I don't think so. Why'd he want to do that?' Huck moved uncertainly towards the door. 'I'm goin' back . . . gonna tell Pa,' he said. 'He don't know what's goin' on . . . not all of it anyway. He'll know what to do about it,' he added, almost as an afterthought.

'I'm sure he will,' Amy muttered, tired, verging on uncaring. But she liked the youngster and his openness, his raw sense of injustice. 'I appreciate what you've done, Huck . . . it couldn't have been easy,' she said kindly.

'You done just fine, kid,' Lenny added. 'There's nothin' gonna happen to Amy or the little 'un. A lot of it, thanks to you.'

Huck grinned manfully. 'I saw your horse – the moro – when I came in. Do you think I could ride him some-time?' he asked.

'Yeah, sure. He ain't goin' anywhere.'

'I'll ride out a-ways with Huck,' Rio said.

As first dark approached, Amy looked up from her rocker. 'I hope that boy isn't headed for a wasted life in Elk Valley,' she said to Lenny.

'I'd say he's headed in the direction *not* to be. Why'd he really ride out here, Amy?'

'That's easy. He's obviously spent most of his young life looking up to Pike Branca. Whatever it was that he got from the man has just been shattered . . . maliciously destroyed. Now he's ridden off hoping to have it all put right by his father . . . and it won't be.'

They sat for a while in silence, listening to the sleepy snufflings of Dub. The soft sounds were coming from the curtained nook at the back of the main room.

Amy's mind was wandering into dark, wretched thoughts. A Butte jury would probably understand, not reach a 'guilty of murder' verdict against her. But if she went back to California, *they* didn't make legal distinctions between honourable men and vermin like Clarkson Chappey.

'I don't want to live in fear of hearing those hoofs pounding up to the front door, Lenny. I want to be like ordinary folk. You know . . . Sunday prayer meetings and picnics by the creek.'

'I ain't ever been hunted, but I've sure wanted to be like them ordinary folk. Difficult when you've got a nice horse an' a brother like Rio.'

They both laughed quietly.

'What you going to do, Amy?' Lenny asked, turning serious.

'Go back to Monterey . . . give myself up.'

'Hmmmm. I thought you'd come up with that,'

Lenny said. 'But it won't achieve anythin'. If you went up in a puff o' smoke, we'd still have to fight for our lives. Don't forget that Stilt and Rio ain't exactly blood brothers. Then there's always Branca and me . . . the moro.' He grinned thinly. 'Besides, you heard Huck say that Stilt was being paid to watch us. Think about it, Amy. Branca wouldn' ride off, if he thought we could leave the valley . . . to go get help from outside.'

Lenny walked to the window, stared into the night. 'No, Amy. From now on, we'll have to fight to get away from here.' He smiled suddenly. 'Sorry, ma'am, but right now I just ain't takin' that risk, You're stayin' home, an' it ain't for the biddin' or pleasure of Pike Branca.'

Amy felt the ripple of a new rapport. 'I can't believe that men are prepared to fight . . . to die over things like this,' she said, in an incredulous whisper.

'They do out here. I seen men . . . fully grown men, gamble on lice racin' around the rim of a hot platter. Then I seen 'em get their meat bags blown out for losin' badly.' Lenny sighed wistfully. 'Horses an' women, Amy. In a country like this, it's what the best fightin's saved up for.'

Amy dragged her fingers slowly through her hair. 'I'll still be wanted by the law, won't I? Nothing's going to change that.'

Lenny pulled off his glove, the one she'd made for his crooked hand. 'Yeah,' he agreed. 'But at least you can afford a good lawyer.'

Amy knew it was a joke, but appreciated the quirk of fate. 'I'm real sorry I lied to you, Lenny. I didn't know how to tell it at the time. Some of us make a real mess of our lives, don't we?' she asked quietly, not expecting a response.

Lenny closed his eyes and leaned back. He reached for his makings and smiled. After a few seconds he answered. 'Yep,' he said. 'We'd better start clearing it up. For a start we'll dig ourselves in here. This is where they all have to come.'

14
Young Gun

Rio decided to go further than he'd intended with Huck. When they got to the wagon road, they doubled back throug the trees. Huck said it would enable them to come in from the north; the barns and outhouses of JUG screening them from the watchful eyes of Furloe Stilt.

If Branca's top hand should catch sight of them, he'd guess where Huck had been and start trouble. Huck wanted nothing more than to see his father, tell him the truth, ask him to intervene as a peacemaker.

A mile from the ranch house they reined in. It was under the bigtooth maple, the same place Huck had left Rio's horse after the incident up in the timber-line.

'No need to follow me in,' he said. 'Stilt's not around . . . can't see anyone else.'

'Oh yeah?' Rio was doubtful. 'What about your pa? You heard Lenny promise nothin' would happen to you.'

Huck thought for a moment. 'He might, twist a bit. But if he listens to what I've got to say, he'll calm down. I'll be all right, Rio.'

'OK kid. I'll just sit here for a while . . . tab with the trees.'

As he drew up to the lamp-lit house, Huck shuddered at the thought of confronting his father. The old man had warned him off going anywhere near Woodside. And if he knew what Pike had been up to behind his back, he'd likely lose his lid.

But Huck believed he was doing the right thing; he'd also told Amy and Lenny what he was going to do. Unobserved, he approached the barn and quickly dismounted, led his horse inside. It was almost black dark, but he had little trouble in unsaddling. He had a glance around him towards the house, then ran for the broad veranda steps.

It looked like the two men who usually took a late-night wander – Malty and Choptank – had already turned in.

For a full minute, Huck crouched under a window. He was listening, getting set. Then he went around the side of the house, let himself in through a narrow door that opened into the kitchen dry-store. He listened again, longer this time, eased himself into the kitchen area proper.

Lights from the main room filtered through the house, and he held his breath as Grange Birdham suddenly walked within three paces of him. Under his breath he cursed with relief as the kitchen door that led out back, slammed to.

Grange Birdham was his father's old-time friend. Had been for ever, it seemed to Huck. He wondered what he'd been doing there. He didn't often come into the house, preferred the outdoors. 'Sunshine an' showers, makes up my hours', Huck had once heard him say.

Huck sensed trouble, could feel it pervading the

close night air. He took a deep breath that almost hurt him, walked into the living-room.

'Hallo Pa,' he said, the tremble from his knees spreading up through his body.

With one foot on the floor and another up, James Genner lay on his leather-covered Chesterfield. In a huge fist, he cradled a quarter-filled glass of whiskey. His head was pitched forward, his heavy jowls resting on his chest. At the sound of Huck's voice he snorted and looked up slowly, his grey eyes pinpointing his young son.

'The cub returns to its den, eh?' he rumbled. 'Frightened of the big, bad world, or had enough of your friends for tonight?'

It took a moment for Huck to understand. 'You got Grange Birdham lookin' out for me? Is that what he's doin' here?' he asked. He held on to the news that Stilt was meant to be doing the same for Pike Branca.

'My men get paid for all sorts o' things. You know that, boy. They're my eyes an' ears.'

Huck matched his pa's heartless look with that of Pike Branca. He knew then his father had no intention of easing up, acting as a peacemaker for his foreman's doings. The frustration and hurt flowed from him. 'They don't start out as that,' he hollered. 'But now I know why you need 'em. You're surrounded by folk you've done wrong to . . . still doin' it.'

Genner dropped his whiskey. In rage, he pounded his fist against his knee. 'Goddammit, boy, you don't talk to me like that. Not in this house.'

But Huck wasn't going to fail. He'd said too much to back down now. '*This house*,' he repeated. 'You mean, *your house* . . . like everything is yours. Well it ain't, an' you can't control it any longer, Pa.' Huck's voice was trembling and his eyes were wet, but he carried on. 'It's all been lies and make-up, Pa. Pike murdered Smiles Macaw, an' you let him off . . . even used the law to do it. You're not God, Pa. Not any longer.'

Genner went rigid with anger, then he swung off his sofa. He looked as though he was ready to rush the walls.

'The Sands ain't leavin',' Huck hit him with, while backing off. 'Why should they? They own that land along Plum Creek . . . own it right and proper. It never was yours, not like all the others that. . . .'

There was so much welling up inside Huck that he suddenly wanted to get away – get some of Birdham's weather in his face. 'You got here first, Pa, an' you're the biggest. But you don't own the valley, no matter how many times you say it. Amy Teague, an' Lenny an' Rio Sand ain't gonna roll over. They're gonna stand up to you and your men.'

From the bearing, the expression of his father, Huck saw the end was near. He got to thinking about what was going to happen next.

Genner had made up his mind about that. 'They send you over here to say that, did they?' he rasped, 'your new sidekicks. Well, you *said* it, son. Now stuff a sack an' get out.'

'Not until I've spoke my bit,' Huck stated, a tad bravely. 'No one sent me here. It's what I know. There's also somehin' *you* should know. It's Pike . . . he. . . .'

'I said, get out,' Genner barked. 'You've flown your colours, an' they ain't on the Genner pole.' He moved heavily forward, and Huck edged to the door.

Huck had expected some smoke, not the rage or vindictive words his father lashed him with. But there was spirit in the youngster, and for a long emotional moment he held his father's gaze. Then with an aquiescent smile he saluted and left the house.

In the cool night air he swore, used words that would certainly have got him a slamming from his Pa. But things had changed. He looked towards the darkness of the distant tree-line, wondered if Rio was still out there. He eyed a pale, frisky horse that was nosing its way around the corral. 'I'm owed that,' he said. 'Outrun the booger men.'

Huck was trembling when, with Rio, he once again approached the Meadow ranch. It was almost dawn, but there was a light, still burning. He sniggered as it went out, told Rio he'd seen the same thing happen on his earlier visit.

From inside the house, Lenny had seen them, was easing back the hammer of his long-barrelled Colt.

'Rio's back, Amy. Looks like he's brought young Huck Genner with him.'

Amy struck a match to relight the lamp. 'Huck?' she questioned. 'What's he come back for?'

'Rio probably got lost . . . he's been long enough.'

'Any room at the inn?' Rio asked, as he came through the door. 'We've got us another recruit.'

Rio was saddle-tired, Huck was exhausted. He was falling asleep as he told Amy and Lenny of the encounter with his father.

When he'd finished, Lenny was very quiet. He knew father-son things like that weren't good.

And Amy knew it of her sister, Freyer, but she broke the affecting silence, 'It's because you're right, Huck. He knew if too, but he didn't know you were grown up enough to tell him so. When he realizes it, he'll come round.'

The heir to JUG rubbed his eyes, shook his head. 'Naah, not Dad . . . not James Genner.' He smiled wearily. 'I've had it with him an' Pike. If you could . . . there's nowhere else I. . . .'

'You can stay here if you want,' Amy cut in. 'There's already one troop decided to stay over. You can make up a pallet in the barn . . . there's just about room.'

Rio winked. 'Welcome to the Plum Creek Volunteer Force,' he said tiredly.

15
A Divided Force

The morning following that night, Grange Birdham brought the news that James Genner didn't want to hear. He rode up to the house on a hot, sweaty horse, dismounted and lumped up the front steps.

'He went straight to the Meadow ranch, Jim,' he reported as Genner stepped on to the veranda. 'One o' the brothers was waitin' for him about a mile out. They rode together. That's four of 'em out there now.'

Genner groped for a suitable oath, brought to mind the face of Amy Teague. His thick knuckles turned white as he gripped the handrail of the stoop. She was the start of his trouble. He could have taken care of the Sand brothers if *she* hadn't turned up. She was a fine-looking woman, and he understood the effect she'd had since arriving from Butte. It looked like Lenny Sand and Pike Branca had been struck by the same thunderbolt.

After she'd refused his offer for Meadow ranch, he decided she'd have to go. He thought he'd leave her to Branca. Let him sort it out – or Lenny Sand. But now?

He knew he'd have to step in, before he lost any more control of those around him.

'Go find Malty,' he said morosely. 'Both of you come in the house. Have some sit-down food.'

Huck was well liked, and Genner wanted to sound out the men's feelings, before paying another less friendly visit to the Meadow ranch. 'Huck bein' out there don't change my plans,' he asserted, as they fingered ribs and eggs. 'And as for Woodside . . . that closes for tradin' some time tomorrow. Huck's chosen his bedfellows. Remember that, when the time comes.'

Genner searched the men's faces for signs of misunderstanding or defiance. He knew they wouldn't like his attitude. Birdham in particular would have a disposition, a commitment to Huck's well being; but nothing was said.

The sun was into its morning climb when Malty brought out Genner's rig. As he backed up the big black mare, he called to Genner. There was a wagon with two men up. It was approaching from the direction of the marshlands to the east. Genner looked out, recognized Pike Branca driving.

He spat into the ground. 'They all come back, some time or other,' he muttered to himself. Genner's heart-rate doubled as he thought of Branca's lusty irrational pursuit of Amy Teague, the stupidity of his placing Furloe Stilt to drygulch Lenny Sand. It was that that had stirred the girl to throw in with the brothers. Genner guessed it was the Branca move that had finally embittered young Huck.

He stepped away from the rig, squared his shoulders. As the wagon drew into the yard, he threw a cursory glance at Milton, decided immediately to ignore him.

He waited until Branca climbed down alongside the corral, then he took a menacing pace forward.

'Where the hell you been?' he asked roughly.

Branca looked wary, uncomfortable. 'We been to the marshes, got some snappers. Would o' got back to the lake for some fish. . . .' He stopped the explanation, saw it was going nowhere. He looked at the detective, back to Genner. 'This is Henry Milton. He's . . .'

Genner cut in. 'I told you one month at the Soak, Pike. Now, are you goin' back while still in my employ or not?'

Branca stared angrily at Genner, Then he calmed down a bit. 'I ain't the doorknob o' this outfit, boss. What's got into you?'

'I told you, goddammit. I've got somethin' to do. Stay away 'til I've done it. I'll let you know when that is.'

Branca nodded sourly. 'Huck's gone, I'm told. Somethin' you said, was it?'

Momentarily, Genner let the brave sarcasm ride. He thought it was for the benefit of the man called Milton. 'Yeah, he's turned against me. Looks like the idiot kid's decided to ride with the Sands and the Teague woman.' He looked icily at Branca. 'Let's hope for your sake, he don't decide to *shoot* with 'em, Pike.'

'What do you mean by that?'

'I hold you responsible. You're gonna take some of the blame for Huck's . . . how shall we say . . . estrangement? And you'll pay for it Pike, if anythin' happens to him. He's messed up by goin' to the Meadow ranch, but you've rode point on it, I'm gonna give 'em one more day out there, then they pack up . . . leave the valley.'

Branca made a slight, curious grin. 'Oh no, boss,' he said. 'Whatever you do, you ain't doin' that. That little flame-head's for me to take care of.'

Malty had hitched up the black. He held on to the traces, shook his head at the inevitable.

'I know you ain't told *her* that, Pike. But when you do, tell it to Lenny Sand, as well.' Genner's grin was very thin, 'You takin' care o' her, you maggot-wit? You got more chance of gettin' muck from a rockin' horse.'

The two men were glaring at each other with anger and defiance. Neither of them paid much attention as Milton climbed from the wagon. Like Malty, he too had sensed Genner was tired of talking.

Genner's voice rumbled into the quiet. 'It'll be Sand or me that sees you dead Pike, if you take up with the Teague girl.'

Branca thought for a second, ran his fingers around his chin. 'An' I'll see *you* dead, Mr Genner, before I'm forced to stop tryin'.'

Branca flashed a look towards Milton, jerked his head sideways. But he was too late to avoid Genner's fist. The big ham came up and across with brutal speed, struck him under the jaw with the force of a piston engine, His feet didn't leave the ground, but it stretched him out. He went down like a poleaxed cow and lay there just as unmoving.

'Pike's body's gettin' to know its place.' For the first time in many weeks, Genner gave a satisfied smile. He didn't give Branca another look, but threw a quick glance at Milton. 'I don't know who the hell you are, mister, but you're on my property,' he said calmly. He tugged at the brim of his Stetson. 'Take back your mount an' get off it. If Branca's thick-headed enough to come to before you're gone, tell him Elk Valley's full. Tell him to find somewhere else.'

Genner nodded once at Malty as he climbed into his rig. He snatched at the reins and the black responded.

He was headed towards Meadow ranch. Dust and small pebbles flew as he swerved from the yard on to the wagon road.

16
Last Warning

The small, Meadow ranch house was surrounded by its home pasture. On all sides, flat grassland stretched for nearly a mile; a distance beyond the effective reach of a rifle bullet. For this reason Lenny and Rio Sand stayed on. They chose it for its defensive advantage because, according to Huck Genner, Pike Branca would come for Dub and Amy Teague.

Lenny made strategic decisions. He took the front, placed Huck and Rio as look-outs to the south and east. From their windows, the angle of view also covered much land to the blind-side north. They held a position that would be hard to overrun; better than Woodside, where the timber-line ran to within fifty yards of the house and outbuildings.

No one knew if Branca had any backing, but Huck said he'd heard Branca tell Milton that a few broke cowboys had been paid a month's wages to join up with him.

In the flat light of early morning, Huck reminded Lenny that Branca was still hell bent on getting the moro. 'He's made you an enemy, Lenny. That's what he does if he wants somethin'. Then he gets people to side with him . . . goads 'em. That's why Stilt's out for Rio. Pike's been ridin' him to get revenge.'

Huck was shaking with callow resentment. He peered out of the window beside Rio. 'It's real complicated, now,' he carried on grimly. 'Pa's mad at me . . . made me pack. But he's furious with Pike . . . I can tell. Pike never told him what he was doin'. That's why Pa's like a horse with a saddle burr.'

Lenny listened, thought for a second. 'Suppose Branca and your pa got to squarin' up,' he put to Huck. 'Not over us . . . me an' Rio or Amy, but over who's lead steer. You said Branca's got some help . . . out o' town men. But who would JUG hands follow?'

'They'd ride with Pa. He's the one who pays 'em. Some of 'em been on JUG a long time. Stilt's the only one who'd join up with Pike.'

Lenny's eyes narrowed. 'Maybe that's all we need. If your pa an' Branca start their own little war, it'll divide the force against us . . . weaken 'em.'

'Don't forget that detective . . . Milton,' Rio chipped in. 'Branca'll see that he flings some lead our way.'

'No I haven't forgot him. Perhaps we can leave him to Amy. She's capable of. . . .' Lenny stopped his near indiscretion. 'We oughta make a round trip to Woodside,' he said. 'We got to let Ed know what we're doin'. We can load a wagon with supplies. Rio wants to be well armed if we're gonna make a stand here.'

Amy nodded as though she though it was a good, practical idea.

After they had gone, time dragged. Amy had to give Dub more play space than the house provided, and it was difficult to keep an eye on him when he wanted to explore beyond the stoop. But ever since the incident in the Silver Grass hotel, Huck had taken to the toddler. As far as Dub was concerned, he'd no less natural caring ability than Amy, so he provided an opportunity for her to check out the state of her ranch.

She tended to small, routine chores, mainly rode close keeping a watchful eye on the north and south boundaries. She began to worry, wondered from what direction Branca and his henchmen would show.

She pondered on her circumstances. She'd never known of greed or hurt or lust for power; that it was often for its own sake. She had no way of knowing that one day she'd be caught in the middle of such a struggle; that she'd be self-appointed guardian to her dead sister's child and men would be shedding blood across her own land.

That was when she remembered her rifle. She'd left it at the south-east corner of the pasture, with the fencing tools. There'd be no immediate need of a claw hammer, but the Winchester was big protection.

She hurried to the small corral and saddled her grey. There could be little danger involved in a mile ride across the pasture and she told Huck as much. She told him to stay near the house, keep an eye on Dub at all times; told him it wasn't far, she wouldn't be gone long. She wasn't reassured by his doubtful look as she rode off.

Not wanting to be surprised or trapped by Branca, Amy was keeping a watchful eye. She saw James Genner approaching from half a mile away, There was no mistaking the big rancher. He was, as always, dressed in black, but this time there was no rig, just the black horse. He was riding hard along the line of the fencing, and Amy took a nervous glance at the distance that separated her from the Winchester. She kicked the grey and decided it would be close run, wondered if she was going to get shot.

She saw the claw hammer first, the glint of light on steel. She leaped from her saddle and took the soft ground on the run, saw the rifle lying in the lush grass. She levered a shell into the breech and took a long look at the oncoming Genner.

She walked to the grey and carefully pulled herself back into the saddle, resolutely turned to face him. Could it be that he was trying to get ahead of Branca, or was he after reconciling himself with his son? Amy smiled wryly. Whichever, the south-east corner of Meadow ranch was certainly one of his favourite meeting places.

Then she saw the two other riders. They were a way behind Genner, but appeared to be giving chase. Genner gave no sign he knew of them and came riding on, making straight for Amy.

She turned the grey side on and levelled the Winchester as Genner approached, felt immediately more nervous as the two back riders suddenly peeled off.

They rode to the west, and in a brief, uneasy flash Amy wondered if Genner was supposed to hold her up there, while the other two headed her off. But they couldn't have known they'd meet her, or anyone else, away from the house.

She looked into Genner's basilisk stare, felt his grey eyes searching for her disposition as he closed in. His big black was snorting, its neck streaked with ribbons of sweaty froth. The cloth of Genner's coat was dry-muddied, as was one of his trouser-legs. To Amy it looked like he'd taken a fall; maybe in his fervour to get to her, if that's where he was going.

Genner *had* taken a fall as he'd veered his horse off the wagon road. But he'd rolled with it, and apart from shaking himself up a bit, only got some bruises. Other than pride, he'd lost no more than five minutes; the time it took the pursuing Branca and Henry Milton to get within a few hundred yards of him.

Amy instinctively recoiled from Genner's livid features, his pent-up anger, as he leaned towards her.

'You think you've beat me on this?' he snarled. 'It'll take more'n that cute-lookin' rifle to stop me.' Genner was using his size to control the excited black. 'I'll use it to show you somethin' that'll make an Apache's eyes water. You'll. . . .'

Genner's threat trailed off in strangled anger and he kicked the black forward. Amy's grey shied away, its eyes bulging with fear.

Amy's heart was pounding, and she screamed. 'Leave me. Leave me and my land. Get away from here,' She still didn't understand what it was that Genner wanted, couldn't understand why, with his anger, he didn't pull a gun.

She swung up the rifle from close range. 'You're trespassing,' she said, almost choking at her stupid pomposity.

She whirled her pony away, fired a single shot into the air. Genner's black reared, stomped its hind legs in a complete circle. She kicked her heels and fired again. It was all she could do, other than shoot him in cold blood as he tried to bear down on her. For a split second, the hotel room in Monterey swam into Amy's thoughts, then she yelled at the grey to run for home.

She fired again, hoping that Huck would secure

himself and Dub inside the house. She hoped that Lenny and Rio would have returned from Woodside, but knew it was too soon. On their return, even with a partly loaded wagon, they'd have to take the wagon road.

At the thought of Genner bearing down on her home and Dub, anger suddenly flared in Amy. She pulled at the reins, kept up the pressure until they came to a standstill. She jumped down and kneeled while the grey walked off a few paces.

Her mouth was parched and her heart thumped uncontrollably as she saw Genner gaining ground. She turned once and looked back towards the house; too late, cursed herself for leaving Dub and Huck on their own.

She aimed, exhaled and pulled the trigger. It was a good shot and she saw Genner flinch as the bullet tore through the upper part of his leg. But nothing more happened. The black was only slowed and Genner urged it on. Amy fired again, at the same spot. 'I'll take your leg right off if you don't go back,' she yelled. She could see the tearing rage across Genner's face, the pain that devastated his body as the second bullet ripped home.

Amy cursed, used some seamen's language she'd got from her sister when she was dying of typhoid. She aimed precisely for Genner's chest, held it there while he advanced. He was so close, she could hear him.

'If I'd wanted to kill you, I could o' done it any time. But I ain't no lady-killer.' Genner took off his hat, breathed deep and painful. 'An' I use the word "lady" very ill-advisedly,' he rasped.

As the black edged ever closer, Amy increased her finger pressure on the trigger. She listened, gripped with Genner's words.

'I just want you out of this valley.' He managed a thin, evil grin. 'Before I turn real nasty. Before I set Allie Macaw and some o' the town bitches on you. That's real trouble.' His words ended with a broken cackle.

It was only because she'd shot dead Clarkson Chappey that she didn't pull the trigger. That, and because Genner was Huck's father.

'Please go back, Mr Genner. Please don't make me shoot.'

The silence was overpowering. Grasshoppers had returned to within inches of where Amy knelt. Other than Genner's faltering breath, they made the only sounds.

Amy was muttering a silent prayer; it was something to stop Genner moving, when the man's chest exploded. It was almost simultaneous with the crash of the rifle shot from behind her. She watched spell-bound, riveted with fear as Genner fell forward. He coughed and raised his head, dropped the reins. His enormous hands opened and closed and he stared without focus. His last few words were low and onerous.

'I shoulda known you'd do it . . . you goddamn murderin' whorebitch.'

Genner grunted once and curled heavily down from the saddle. He landed with a dull thud and Amy thought the ground moved a little. She got to her feet, and when she turned, she just glimpsed a dun horse cantering beyond the fence line. The rider was crouched low, but still familiar to Amy as he made for the distant line of timber.

She shook her head, stared towards the house. Anyone smart enough to be keeping a look-out, anyone who'd heard the shooting would have had a view. Only it hadn't happened the way it looked.

She walked towards her horse, snatched furiously at its reins. She rammed the rifle behind the saddle skirt, looked up to see Huck already racing through the pasture towards her. Swearing again, she went back to Genner's body, waited to face the anguish of his young son.

17
Bloody Land

At the first crack of the Winchester, Huck quickly but gently pushed Dub under his cot. He grabbed his own gun and rushed for the door. He stopped, was standing with his back to it, breathing fast, when he heard the second shot echo across the pasture. He lifted the latch and stepped outside, his eyes darting around for signs of movement. He saw it, gasped with relief when he saw his father riding steadily towards Amy. They were almost midway between the yard gate and the fence line, but even from that distance, Huck could see that Genner's advance on Amy was menacing.

He called out and waved his arms when he saw Amy turn back and kneel, aim her rifle. He was running swift and reckless when he heard the next shot, saw his pa crumple forward and fall to the ground.

He was yelling frantically as he staggered to where his father lay. He stared down, his lungs heaving. 'I saw. I was with Dub. He's . . . he's in the house . . . I. . . .'

'I didn't shoot him, Huck,' Amy stuttered. 'It wasn't me who fired that shot.' Amy let go of her rifle and held out her hands.

They both looked towards Genner, then back at each other.

'He's dead, ain't he?' Huck said heavily.

'Yes,' Amy gulped. 'The things he said to me, Huck. Why? What have I done?'

'You were shootin' him, Amy.'

Amy was shaking. 'I shot him to make him stop. The last shot . . . it came from behind me. That's what killed him. It wasn't me.'

They both looked across the pasture towards the fence line, where it cornered at the edge of the trees. It was silent and still, not even a sparrow stirred.

Amy turned back to the house, got to her feet. 'What did you do with Dub?' she asked, suddenly frightened again.

'He's OK. I shut the door.'

But Amy was hardly listening, she was staring back at the timber-line. She knew there was a killer somewhere in the trees; had no proof he'd gone. 'We've got to get back to the house . . . try an' take your pa,' she said, trying to conceal her fear.

They both had tears running down their faces, found breathing difficult as they lifted Genner's body from the blood-soaked grass; as they pushed and pulled the torpid body across the saddle of the big black.

Amy was desperate to get back to the house and Dub. But with Huck there, she couldn't leave Genner. It took them many minutes to complete the grisly task, then, with Huck leading the black and Amy her grey, they stumbled their way back to the house.

As they went through the gate into the yard, Huck asked Amy if she'd seen anything after the last shot had hit his pa. 'I saw you lookin', Amy. You looked behind you. What did you see?'

'I just saw . . . heard. But it doesn't matter, Huck. Whoever fired that shot will blame it on me. Even *you* can't deny I shot him. I can't prove I didn't kill him.'

Huck didn't want to push it; part of him didn't want to know any more. But it sounded as though maybe Amy had seen something. 'You won't have to, Amy,' he said. 'They'll have to prove you *did*. I know that. And I believe you, so I'll lie about some of it.'

Huck's mind was racing with despair and doubt. He knew that with his pa dead, Pike Branca would be the turnkey, the new ruler of Elk Valley, regardless of what was or wasn't proved, or who owned JUG Ranch.

As soon as they got close to the house, Amy ran for the door.

'I'm going after Lenny and Rio,' she said, as soon as she'd made sure Dub was safe; after they'd manhandled Genner's bloody body into the screened alcove which was Amy's bedroom.

For a long while Huck sat staring at his father, the bloodied chest and leg, the ashen, grizzled head. He held out a switch, pushed and pulled it mindlessly as Dub responded to the tugging game.

'You crying, Huck?' the child asked solemnly.

Huck sniffed. 'No. It was the wind and the sand . . . the dust.'

'The man's crying,' the child said, pointing at Genner's body.

Huck grinned sadly. 'Yeah,' he said, 'the man's cryin'.' Then he leaped to his feet when his father emitted a long, low sigh.

James Genner wasn't dead. The big, tough rancher had the constitution of a bear.

Huck poked around for clean cloths and water. Then

he carefully cut away the sticky torn suiting, blanching when the man's eyes fluttered. To the best of his ability, he cleansed and bandaged his father's wounds. Huck had seen young cows caught on wire being sowed up and foals being born, but this was the first time he'd had his fingers coloured by warm blood. The fact that it was his own father returned from the dead made him feel queasy and very lonely.

He was swallowing hard, looking at the chest wound when he heard the sound of the rear door being opened. He reached out and pulled Dub towards him. Rigid, he listened to movement, hushed voices in the scullery. He stood silent and looked round the room for his rifle, remembered he'd propped it outside the front door.

He groaned wretchedly when Pike Branca and Henry Milton stepped into the room.

'What the hell you doin' here, kid?' Branca snarled. 'Where's Amy?'

'You know'd I was here . . . know'd Rio, an' Lenny Sand are here as well. Stilt must've told you. You paid him to keep watch on everyone. I heard you.'

'You heard me?' Branca took a threatening step forward.

Huck was suddenly afraid. With his uncontained, raw anger, he'd trapped himself. 'I was in the house when you came in with him,' he said, nodding towards Milton. 'I heard everythin' you said about Amy.'

Branca rubbed his chin, looked dangerous. 'Where's Amy?' he snarled again.

'You paid Stilt to tell you that not me,' Huck retorted staunchly.

Branca's eyes moved around the room until he found what he was looking for. A nasty look crossed his face when he saw Genner's body partly screened on the bed behind Huck. 'She must o' helped you get your pa back here. Least she could do after killin' him,' he said.

'How'd you know she killed my pa?' Huck asked. 'You been that close?'

As he was thinking about his response, Milton cut in. 'That's right. From a distance, but we saw her . . . saw her shoot.'

Huck shuffled sideways. He wanted to draw their attention away from the bed, hoped Genner didn't make any more noise. 'If you saw it, you know Amy never killed him,' he said. 'He was still ridin'. She fired to stop him comin' on. That last shot was from . . .' Huck stopped, looked quickly from Milton to Branca.

'You're overexcited kid. Your head's a little muddled. She'd never've warned him, an' there was no last shot other than hers,' Milton said. He waited while Huck thought about what he was saying, then, while Branca cast another glance at Genner, Milton continued:

'This woman you know as Amelia Teague. Murder ain't exactly an original sin to her. I've been on her trail for months. The nubbin' here . . .' he gestured towards Dub, 'he's Dub Chappey, not Horley . . . but he's her nephew all right. She shot Dub's father in cold blood . . . from real close up. Then she fled north, taking the child with her.' Milton looked concernedly at Huck. 'It's his grandparents, Huck. They want him, and they're payin' me to bring him back.'

Huck's chest was heaving, and he was shaking his head with exhaustion. As though Dub sensed a deadlock he stood in the middle of the room, looking from face to face.

Huck desperately wanted Amy to come back with Rio and Lenny. 'No,' he burst out. 'I heard you, remember?

You were in my house, an' I heard it all . . . what you were goin' to do.'

Branca laughed. 'Bein' a kid's wasted on you, Huck. You're smart, but I wish I'd known at the time you were earwiggin'.'

Milton had been thinking. 'Then Hannah . . . Amy, knows I'm here? Here in Fishtail?' he demanded of Huck.

'Yeah, she knows. So do Rio an' Lenny. When they get back they'll . . .'

'When they get back, we'll be waitin' for 'em. That's the neck end of it, kid,' Branca sneered quickly at Huck's warning.

At each short silence, Huck strained his ears for the slightest sound of anyone returning. He'd been anxious to prove himself a worthy supporter of Amy and the Sand brothers, but now it seemed he'd failed them utterly.

Milton seemed to sense Huck's thoughts and stepped to one side, looked sidelong through the front window. 'Why risk everything by staying, Pike?' he asked. 'This little feller's worth half the Cornish spread or a small fortune from Clarkson Chappey's old man . . . maybe, both. If we left now, we'd have him an' our hides intact. What do you say?'

Huck retreated a step, pulled Dub in beside him. 'You can't do this, Pike. None of us have done anythin' to you. Amy said she'd set the hounds of hell on you, if anything happens to Dub.'

'The hounds of hell, eh?' Branca aped. Then he looked hard and quick at the detective. 'Yeah, maybe . . . I dunno,' he said, turning on Huck.

Clutching firmly at Dub, Huck backed off. The child felt the tense grip against his shoulders and whimpered. Within moments the two of them were pressed against the far wall of the room.

'Quit the brat cryin',' Branca threatened as he crowded them.

Huck moved himself in front of Dub. 'Go on Pike, hit me. If you like, you can start on Dub. Get the detective to help when it's my turn.'

Branca snorted then lashed out with the flat of his hand. Huck could hardly believe it, was too late to avoid the infuriated movement.

The blow caught him heavily across his face and everything inside his head seemed to burst. Then Branca caught him again and he blinked against the shock, fought the stinging lights of pain and being beaten.

Dub gave a muffled cry and Huck wanted to protect him, fight back. But there wasn't time, and he closed his eyes as he swung futilely at Branca.

18
Broken Family

At Woodside, Lenny and Rio were loading their freight wagon when Amy rode in at the gallop. Lenny was hefting a box of Edwards's healing potions.

'What's happened?' he yelled, seeing the sweat along the grey's flanks.

'It's Genner ... he's dead.' Hardly pausing for breath, Amy then retold the events out at Meadow Ranch. 'I lied to Huck,' she concluded. 'I told him I didn't see anyone when I looked back. But I did. I saw a dun horse, and I recognized the rider. I know who shot Genner, Lenny, but I couldn't tell Huck.'

'Pike Branca,' Lenny said forcefully.

'Yes. The man he'd looked up to for all those years, shot his father.' Amy remained sitting her horse. She looked tired and distressed. 'What's happening in this valley, Lenny?' she asked.

'What we goin' to do about it, that's what I want to know,' Rio anxiously broke in. 'Huck's alone there with Dub ... for the second time,' he murmured, but Amy heard him.

'We'll leave all this ... just take the ammo an' Ed's

132

medicines.' Lenny glanced at Amy. 'We can't have you fightin' a second murder charge, can we?' he said. 'We've got to get through to Sheriff Gane . . . let him know what's goin' on here.'

The three riders slowed to a canter and Lenny pulled the moro to a halt. Amy and Rio rode alongside, stirrup to stirrup.

'Notice anything odd?' Lenny asked.

'No . . . not yet . . . should we?' Rio answered, slow and thoughtful.

'Yeah. Huck ain't much more'n a kid. Don't you think he'd be out of the door, shoutin' wavin', doin' somethin'?'

'Yeah, you're right. I would be.'

'Huck!' Rio immediately yelled across the pasture. 'Huck, where are you?'

When no answer came, Rio kicked his horse into a hesitant trot and Amy and Lenny followed. Rio swung down on to the steps, was first through the door and into the main room. He saw Huck and stepped quickly forward, his eyes darting warily around him.

As Amy and Lenny pushed in behind him, he turned to face them. 'He'll live,' he said. 'Looks like he took a slap in the chops.'

Amy levered a pan of water from the kitchen pump, and within seconds Huck was grimacing, grousing faintly.

'Where's Dub, Huck? Where's Dub?' Amy demanded.

Lenny stared around him, took notice of Rio who nodded towards Amy's bed. He saw Genner's body, looked back to Amy.

'Huck, come on,' she pleaded. 'Please, Huck. Tell

me where Dub is. What happened? Huck . . . Huck.'

Huck moved his jaw. 'Took him . . . they took him . . . Pike,' he groaned.

'Branca,' Amy whispered sickeningly.

'Yeah. Him an' that detective, Milton.' Huck tried to sit up. 'I told him we knew what he was doin'. He wanted to wait here for you. Milton said to take Dub . . . come back with . . .' Huck drank some of the water from the pan. 'I tried to stop 'em, Amy.'

Lenny nodded. 'We know you did, Huck. It ain't your fault.'

Amy looked at Lenny, uncomfortably.

'Don't worry. You couldn't o' won that one,' Rio muttered.

Amy got to her feet. Angrily she made for the front door, but Lenny stepped in, grabbed her arm.

'That ain't gonna get the kid back, Amy. It's what Branca wants,' he said, letting go of her. 'Dub's safe in their hands for a while. To Milton, he represents some years of good living, an' Branca can only manipulate you through Dub. We'll get him back, Amy. I swear to you.'

Rio exchanged an unconvinced looking glance with his brother.

'Yes, all right,' Amy said. 'Tell me what you think we should do then.'

Before Lenny could answer her, a low, rumbling cough came from the bed. They all stared at each other for a moment, then turned towards Genner. Rio pulled aside the partly screening curtain and they saw Genner's throat pulsating, his head twisted towards them.

Lenny's jaw dropped, Amy mouthed silent words of shock.

'Looks like he's tired o' bein' dead,' Rio quipped.

'Your pa ain't dead. You hear me?' Lenny asked Huck.

Huck struggled to his knees. 'I knew,' he said, 'I did what I could . . . looked like he was dyin'.'

Amy had turned her attention, and the water, on to Genner. She was bathing his sweating, colourless face. The man's pain was evident, but with an iron will, Amy thought, death could be days away instead of what looked like minutes.

'If one of us could . . .' Amy started to say, but a gasping stutter from the rancher interrupted her.

'No one . . . no one else. She did it . . . . murderin' trash,' Genner managed, before lapsing into his embittered oblivion again.

Distressed, Amy got to her feet, moved back a pace.

Lenny stepped forward. He thought Genner looked very old and harmless, weighed that against all the suffering he'd caused in the valley.

'He knows who it was shot him,' Huck said, standing shakily. 'But he's tryin' to convince himself it was Amy. The youngster rubbed his hands across his face. 'He can't believe he could be so wrong about Pike. But he's dyin' and it *was* Pike that shot him. We all know it except him.'

'Yeah, maybe, Huck,' Lenny said. 'But we got to think on.' Lenny looked to Rio. 'One of us has got to get to Billings,' he suggested. 'We can't leave Genner here . . . or can we?' He grinned. 'We've got to get the doc from Fishtail, so I guess it's you or me, brother.'

'Then it'll be me,' Rio stated. 'Seein' as how you've worked twenty pounds off me at Woodside, I'll run out the moro. Anyways, you'll be back in your sick bed if you go horse-racin' across the basin.'

Lenny considered arguing, but couldn't think of a way of winning other than busting his brother's head. It *was* going to be a long, hard ride and there couldn't be any waiting for the cover of darkness.

Amy's house could be well defended, and any opposition would be in the open. But unless Rio got through and made it to Billings, they'd all most probably die.

A short while later, Lenny shoved a rifle into Rio's saddle boot. 'Keep to the trees for as long as possible. Don't say nothin' to no one, you hear?' Lenny warned his brother.

'How's he meant to do that when he gets to town . . . when he wants to find Chillum?' Amy asked. 'Remember the trouble I had?'

The two men exchanged a droll glance. Rio winked and leaped into the saddle. He nudged the moro and within five minutes he'd cleared the pasture on his ride to Fishtail.

19

Ready and Waiting

Soon after Rio Sand made the safety of the tree-line, Pike Branca rode the same trail to Meadow Ranch pasture.

Within the house, the three defenders had made themselves ready. All had a rifle apiece with ammunition brought from Woodside and Lenny had his .44 revolver.

From a slot in the front door, Lenny watched five riders swing towards the ranch outbuildings. 'Branca's comin',' he said, calmly. 'Looks like he might o' got some help from town. Amy, you an' Huck keep watch from back an' the south. I'll cover the front. Let's hope none of 'em have circled north.'

'I wager they never even caught sight of Rio,' Amy speculated, as if reading Lenny's mind.

The men got closer, but looking uncertain as to what to expect from the house, Branca halted them at the yard gate. Lenny suddenly realized he'd let them get too close and alerting Huck and Amy, he deliberately fired a bullet into a fence post. It was less than three feet from one of the horsemen.

He swore silently as the riders turned, rode back a safe distance. He swore again as he watched Branca break from the bunch, advance once again on the house.

He levered another round into the breech, called out as Branca walked his horse through the gate. 'I ain't blind or deaf Branca. State your business from there. I'm comin' out.'

'You stay here, Lenny. You can't trust him. What about us?' Amy protested.

'He knows I've got to step outside Amy. He won't try anythin'. Without cover he knows his chances of gettin' even half-way across the pasture are nil . . . even if they put a bullet in me.'

Lenny pulled back the door and edged on to the veranda, swung up the barrel of the rifle.

Branca laughed. 'How's Mr Genner?' he mocked.

Lenny thought for a second. 'Still livin'.'

Branca glared back at him 'It's him I come to talk to, Sand.'

'You ain't foolin' anyone here, Branca,' Lenny said harshly. 'Just tell us what you've done with Dub.'

'He's safe. Let me talk to Amy . . . see her.'

'You'll live longer talkin' to me, Branca.'

Branca's face darkened. 'You tell her, I'll buy Milton off. Tell her the kid'll be safe in the valley. I'll say, whoever shot Mr Genner got away . . . never even identified.'

Lenny whistled through his teeth. 'You really are as stupid as you look. Branca. You've had your time. Now get off this land.'

Branca stepped his horse forward threateningly. 'You're through, Sand. You an' your brother. Turn the moro over to me and I'll let you leave with all you can load on that old freighter of yours. Huck can go along, but Amy stays with me.'

Lenny stepped back against the front door. 'There ain't a louse would stay with you,' he said.

Branca wheeled his horse in a tight circle. 'I'm givin' you all a chance,' he snarled. 'Take it or leave it.'

'I guess we'll just have to leave it,' Lenny countered, putting the rifle to his shoulder. 'Talkin' o' chances, Branca. You're takin' a big one in gettin' back to the trees. Stayin' in the saddle with half a dozen bullets in you.'

For a moment Branca sat wondering, estimating Lenny's threat. Then he grinned and spurred the dun.

'He's going back to the JUG,' Huck said to Amy, when he saw Branca ride away.

Lenny came in and shut the door. He'd waited, watched while the men who remained argued. The one who'd obviously drawn the short straw stayed just beyond the gate, and one rode to the east. The third man appeared to swing north, and the fourth cantered his horse to the edge of the south pasture.

'They'll keep us corralled until Branca gets back,' Lenny told them, quietly. He saw them look at him, realized their need, their right to get involved. 'From now on, if you see as much as a shadow, throw some lead. At least we can make 'em think there's four of us.'

They stood alert, nervy in the silence, listening to the breathing of Genner. Lenny knew it wasn't the death rattle, but it wasn't far off.

Branca's man out front wasn't much of a threat, nor was the one who went north. Lenny was more worried about the men who'd ridden east and south.

He'd worried right. The first bullet slashed through

the shutter that Huck had eased open to look from the rear of the house. He was instantly stung with splinters and shards of glass. The shot was more than tentative, it was followed by a measured fusillade from south and west. Most of the bullets went into the logged walls, a few ripped into the chinking, some smacked through the window shutters.

A lamp was blasted from its hanging. It showered Lenny with oil, the glass chimney narrowly missing his neck and face. He dropped to the floor, shouted: 'Down. Get away from the windows.' He heard the clank of kitchen pots and pans as they were smashed from their shelves in the scullery.

Huck grinned maniacally, waved that he was OK.

'What do we do?' Amy cried out.

'Don't know, but do it lyin' down!' Lenny yelled, through the clamour and clash of bullets. He looked towards Genner.

But Amy was there already. 'He's all right,' she said. 'At least, he's still breathing.'

Lenny grunted in acknowledgement, moved over to Amy's window and lifted his rifle. There was a chance that one of the men who'd fired would want to have a look, see his worst. He did, peering around the bole of a felled pine.

He presented a fine, still target and Lenny tut-tutted as he drew a bead, squeezed the trigger.

The rifleman took Lenny's bullet high in his chest. He flew up like a startled prairie chicken, shrieked, then collapsed across the broad stump. His ally called out a name, then pumped bullets back at the south-facing side of the house.

Lenny whirled away from the window with his back to the wall, beckoned for Amy and Huck to keep low.

After half a minute he nodded, indicated that they return the fire.

The three of them poured a torrent of fire across the pasture, coughed and spluttered as hanging gunsmoke spiked their eyes and throats.

Huck called out shakily, 'You all right?'

Lenny looked over at Amy and winked. 'Yeah we're still all all right kid, But one o' them won't be drawin' any more pay.'

'The one out back's been quiet too,' Huck said, 'I think he's moved north where we can't hit him.'

'Yeah, him an' the one out front,' Lenny added. 'I want to take a look at your pa, Huck,' he went on. 'Come an' cover this side, but keep your nose out the way. Remember you can't see snakes in the grass.'

Huck crawled over to the front of the house, and in similar style Lenny moved to the bed, flinching a little when he saw Genner staring up at him. The balsam that Amy had pressed into his chest wound had obviously relieved some of the pain and Lenny saw the man concentrate when he leaned in close.

'You don't want to miss all the fun, do you, Genner?' Lenny said. 'You in much pain?'

'No . . . don't feel a thing. What's goin' on out there?' the rancher grated.

Lenny ducked as a bullet smacked into the wall above Genner's head. He smiled. 'Well, it ain't the harvest festival. It's your foreman. Some of his . . . *your* men have got us cornered until he gets back with the JUG outfit. He's taken over, Genner. So what do you think they've got in mind for us, when they get here, you miserable son of a bitch?'

Genner glowered, and for a moment Lenny thought he was making a move to retaliate.

'Don't know what this stinkin' mess is, you've plugged me with,' Genner said. 'You hope it's gonna keep me alive . . . so's that murderin' hussy won't have to face another murder charge?'

'It's warm rat-shit . . . an' it's meant to kill you,' Lenny hissed. 'You know it was Branca shot you, Genner. Huck knows it . . . we all know it.'

Lenny looked around to make sure Amy and Huck couldn't hear, bent in close to Genner's ear. 'If my brother ain't back with the sheriff before Branca gets here, I'll make sure no one keeps you alive,' he whispered. 'I'll tie a sack around you an' poke the rat in. You got any idea what it'll do to get out, Genner?'

The long, deep-orange rays of sunset were shining on the pine and aspen when Lenny saw the incoming riders. 'They're here,' he said.

Two . . . five . . . seven. He counted uneasily as they swung from west to north. With two or three already hidden somewhere between the house and the trees, Branca had maybe nine men with him now. Lenny wondered if Amy and Huck would appreciate the maths, the odds. Then he wondered how long it would be before Rio got there.

He knew Branca would be expecting four rifles to defend the house, hoped it would make them less aggressive. With only three sides to the house having apertures to fire from, three guns could appear to be more. With fast straight shooting, and if the ammunition held out, it could give them the whip hand.

As the riders wheeled off, Lenny called to Amy: 'They might try to get round to the back corner. If they do, stop 'em. My guess is they'll regroup and come in head on. Huck, you know what to do.'

'Yeah, leave the turkey-shoot to you if they come from the front,' Huck shouted back; the disappointment clear in his voice.

Lenny shook his head, looked along his sight as Branca and his men galloped at the front of Amy's house. He swore, cursed the world and set his mind to gunfire.

The riders spread out and Lenny couldn't get a good shot. Within seconds his left hand hurt bad, and his side wound throbbed as each shot recoiled viciously into his shoulder. His teeth cracked together and the forefinger of his right hand started to bleed. He cursed and shouted for Rio and his scatter-gun to hurry up, as again the acrid smoke hurt his eyes and throat.

Then Amy and Huck joined in as three, then four of the riders attempted to ride around the house away from Lenny's deadly barrage.

A JUG man dived from his saddle, rolled over and over before ending in a tattered, lifeless heap. 'Hunt dirt,' Lenny muttered, his rifle smoking hot in his hands. He was bleeding from his chin and lip where flying splinters had slashed at him.

'Got one,' Huck yelled. 'Looks like a town jackleg.'

The loss of two more men was enough for Branca to ease off his attack and Lenny slumped down with his back against the wall. He reached for more cartridges, crammed them into the loading slot of his rifle. 'I've forgotten what this is all about,' he muttered. 'All I know is . . . young Dub's a lot safer than any of us.'

He swallowed hard, put the gun aside, for a moment. He fumbled for the makings of a cigarette. 'What's goin' on out there?' he asked.

Huck was watching a riderless horse running for the

trees, 'Looks like they're headin' west . . . out front again,' he said.

Amy made a strange choking cry from her south window.

Huck shouted and Lenny threw himself forward on to his elbows, fearful that she'd been hit. 'Amy . . . you all right?' he gasped.

'Yes, I'm not hit. It's . . . it's one of those men. He was close . . . trying to get round back.'

'Yeah, what about him?' Lenny got to his feet, looked to where Amy had pointed. He saw a man crawling towards an empty water-butt. 'Yellow legs. Must be the man from Monterey. Now you've shot a detective, goddammit, Amy.'

Amy turned to face Lenny, her face tight and deathly pale. 'No . . . not him. That's Dub's father . . . Clarkson Chappey,' she said, breathless.

In the abrupt silence that followed, Lenny thought he saw a thin smile flick across Amy's face and he wondered if she really was a killer. 'You're pleased . . . relieved that he . . . Chappey ain't dead yet? Why . . . I don't understand?'

'Pleased . . . relieved?' Amy's eyes were blue fire. 'Of course I am, Lenny. Don't you see? It means he's the one who's been trailing me. There never was anyone called Henry Milton from Monterey. He lied to Branca. Perhaps he did the same about the murder charge.'

Lenny looked at Huck who was trying to make sense of their predicament, mutely trying to understand. 'Yeah,' he said. 'That'd make more sense of any deal he's made.' He got to his feet, looked out of the window. Chappey had got beyond the water-butt. Now he lay still, fifty yards away from the house.

'That buckboard still out back, Amy?' Lenny asked.

'Yes.'

'Your little grey out there?'

'Yes. In the lean-to. Why?'

'We've got to find out where Dub is. If Chappey ain't dead yet, I'll make him tell us.'

Amy opened her mouth, but didn't, couldn't dispute Lenny's pitch.

'I was sort of hopin' you might try and stop me,' he said hopefully. Then he sniffed, smiled. 'But I guess they won't be expectin' me. I'll probably get to him before they realize what's happenin'.'

'What happens when you do . . . get to him?'

'You an' Huck start shootin'. Use up all the ammunition if you have to.'

Lenny made himself lean as he eased through the back door. He was lucky that on that east side, he might be partly screened from the north by the corner of the house.

After hurriedly hitching up Amy's grey, he swerved the buckboard south, keeping the house between him and Branca's riders. He'd almost made up the ground when a startled yell went up.

Three of the riders raced across the north pasture to bring him within range and sighting of their rifles. But from the house, Amy and Huck were ready and laid down heavy fire in an effort to hold them back.

When Lenny reached Chappey, he swung the side of the buckboard against the north pasture. The man wasn't dead and Lenny managed to heft the body into the seat. That's when there was a concerted effort to stop him. Bullets ripped chaotically at the buggy, and Lenny swore, grinned at the twist of fate.

If Branca knew who Lenny had aboard, he'd be one of those firing at him. Branca wouldn't pass up the opportunity to put more bullets into the man he knew as Henry Milton. To his thinking, if Amy had decided to stay, make a fight of it, he didn't need a well-informed detective spoiling his plans.

As Lenny crawled up on to the driving seat, instant fire seared his ribs. But he knew his body hadn't taken a bullet and he yelled, jerked the lines for the grey to turn and run.

He ran the buckboard wildly all the way to the back door of the house and Huck helped him drag the sagging body through into the scullery while Amy covered them from the south window.

'Lenny, are you all right?' she called.

'Yeah, of course. Keep an eye on this man, Amy. If he's who you say he is, he's still your brother-in-law. I've got a bit of cleanin' up to do,' he told her.

'They've made a gather,' Amy said, as she walked into the scullery. 'I think they're about to surrender.'

'Yeah, an' I'm Tom Noddy.'

Amy took a step forward, peeled back the cloth that Lenny was holding to his side.

'Just another flesh wound,' he assured her as he shoved an arm back in his shirt. 'Chappey's the one who ain't gonna recover. If he's to talk, though, I want Genner to hear it. He still with us?'

'Yes. He said something to Huck just now. Said there was no sense in this fight.'

'Oh yeah. He wanted us to give in, did he?' Lenny said, scornfully.

Lenny dragged Chappey close to the bed Genner was lying in. He stepped back as Amy kneeled by his side.

Chappey's eyes opened as she bent over him. 'That red hair . . . it's a killer, Hannah Cornish,' he said, painfully.

Amy almost smiled, and it seemed enough to bring Chappey around for a few minutes; enough for him to tell his tale. He told them what had happened when he'd recovered consciousness from the shooting.

Apparently, he'd convinced the law in Monterey that he'd been in an accident. Out of idle curiosity, he'd been examining Amy's gun in her hotel room. But he was unfamiliar with the action and shot himself. He knew it was the only chance he had to get what he wanted. He'd claimed Amy had panicked, went on the run, lest she be charged with his murder. The law remained sceptical, but in the light of no other evidence, dropped the indictment.

As soon as he was well enough, he set out to trail her, posing as detective Henry Milton. 'It's the badge . . . it helps people to speak,' he said.

Chappey was sweating with the pain of talking, but he closed his eyes and carried on. 'I had to find you . . . to get Dub . . . found out Branca wanted you. That way was better . . . I decided . . .'

'Where's Dub? Where's the little 'un?' Lenny cut in hard.

Chappey heard Lenny. His eyes opened but they held Amy's, 'JUG . . . called Chop . . . sent him there,' he stuttered. His eyes opened for a moment, clouded then closed again. 'Bet it was Branca that shot me . . . same as he did Genner.' The sailor from Monterey smiled despairingly. 'Can't trust no one any more,' he groaned.

Amy turned her head away, and Lenny took the blanket from Genner. The rancher's eyes were closed, but he was feigning oblivion; pretending not to have heard Chappey's final words.

Lenny covered Chappey with the blanket, helped

Amy to her feet. 'He didn't know much about hasty trust,' he said.

'What's to know about it?' Amy asked very quietly.

'It usually brings hasty repentance.'

'He never put any trust in my sister. We're all free of him now,' was Amy's response.

Lenny thought for a second, then turned to Huck. 'Is there someone called Chop out at your ranch . . . your pa's ranch?' he asked.

'Choptank, the old wrangler. There's no need to worry about Dub any more, if that's where they've taken him, Amy. When we get out of this, he'll be ridin' bareback, whoopin' it up.'

'Just like us,' Lenny ribbed.

'That's right, Lenny,' Huck said, ' 'cause I think they're gettin' ready to hit us again.'

Lenny swore violently, leaped for the south window. The Branca force were scattering. It was obvious they were having one more attempt to surround the house before nightfall.

'They'll work their way north to come in on our blind side, an' they'll try an make the sheds,' Lenny figured aloud. 'Heads down time, *amigos*.'

'That's real helpful, Lenny. How about something to boost our confidence?' It was tongue-in-cheek from Amy, but the emotion cracked her voice.

'Rio'll be here in a minute with the cavalry,' he offered.

20
Saved

With first dark, a nervous chill pervaded the house at Meadow Ranch. They were never going to light any lamps, but a hunter's moon was coming to the aid of the plucky defenders. It broke open a night that would have teemed with Branca's menace. Long before midnight, the surrounding pasture was turned to blue day.

'Not even a pocket mouse could sneak up on us tonight,' Huck said, confidently.

'No, but a bullet might. Keep your head down,' Lenny said. 'At least we can hold 'em off if they do try anythin' . . . as long as our ammo lasts,' he added.

'That's the problem, Lenny,' Amy interrupted. 'I'm down to a handful of shells. Unless you've got any more?'

'No . . . no, I haven't,' Lenny said. 'I'm sorry. I brought all we had from Woodside. Me an' Rio always reckoned on ranchin' . . . not gunfightin'.'

Lenny immediately felt regret for his comment. It sounded as though he was resentful at being involved in Amy's predicament, and he wasn't.

'Beaten at last?' came the voice from behind them. 'Soon you'll have nothin' to fight for.' Though James Genner's voice was weak, it still held the tone of arrogance.

'We're fightin' to keep us alive, Genner . . . you included. If we gave up, do you think Branca would let you talk to your men . . . start givin' orders again?' Lenny shook his head. 'No. Genner, your trusty foreman would be the first to put a bullet into you . . . another one, that is. Did you hear what the bogus detective said, before he died?'

'Whoever he is, he's a liar,' Genner charged. 'I've known Pike Branca . . . known him well. There's some things don't . . . can't change a man.'

Huck looked over at his father. 'You're wrong, Pa,' he said. 'When Sheriff Gane gets here, you'll find out. That's where Rio went . . . to get him.'

At first light, a lone rider emerged from the trees on the western side of the pasture. The man turned to the north and Lenny noticed the extra horse he was leading. A shiver ran down his spine and his eyes ached from the staring, He watched the first stream of early light rippling on the withers of his moro. The stallion was being led by Furloe Stilt.

Lenny punched the wall with his fist. 'Rio,' he said thickly, and a crushing bitterness filled him.

Whatever fate had befallen Rio, Branca and his men now knew there were only three in the house, and one of them no more than a kid. With Stilt, they were a lot more worthy of an attack from Branca, Lenny thought.

The timing was perfect as Amy asked, 'Do you think they're going to rush us again?'

'As sure as God made lil' green apples, ma'am.'

Amy was near to despair. 'I'm sorry Lenny . . . Huck,' she said. 'It's because of me, that you're here . . . in this mess.'

'No problem,' Lenny replied. 'Me an' Huck talked it over. Everybody's got to be somewhere, so why not here.'

Branca had lost men and would be angered at having been repulsed by such a small opposing force. Lenny understood that, and he held the front door open an inch. He knew they'd be coming in from the north-west corner and he placed Huck at the window alongside him. Amy took the window beside the back door.

When the attackers rode in, there was no time to aim or search out a target. The three defenders simply fired at will, used up their ammunition. Lenny recognized one or two of the men. Huck was right, they were punchers, broke drifters from Fishtail. They swarmed into the yard, thrashed the ducks from their shallow pond water, trampled vegetables in Amy's garden.

Lenny kicked the door to, and threw down his empty rifle, grabbed at his Colt. From the direction of the wagon road he'd seen more horsemen. They were moving fast and headed in their direction. 'Hold your fire,' he yelled. 'We need to talk this through. We're in real trouble at last.'

'Yes. We're right out of bullets,' Amy agreed.

Lenny shook his head against the continuing noise from outside. 'No, it's not that,' he mumbled, clicking the cylinder of his gun.

He hoped to see caught-up faces, but instead saw Amy staring across the room, her mouth open in astonishment. He even watched as her arm came up, finger pointing. He pulled back the hammer of the Colt and dropped to his knees, his clasped hands bringing the long-barrelled gun up to bear on the form of Genner.

He gasped, shook with disbelief at Genner who was standing beside the bed. As the three of them watched enthralled, the stricken man grasped the back of a chair in one huge hand and took a step forward. It was unbelievable to see him stand, let alone walk. It was the legendary quality of the man that he should still want to control everything around him.

Lenny straightened when he heard boots stomping on the veranda. He moved to one side as the door crashed open, his eyes remaining fixed on the looming figure in front of him.

It was that apparition; the big face sweated with pain, the wad of bloody bandages, the gory, tattered black clothing, that stopped Branca in his tracks as he came through the door.

Lenny turned and saw Branca's terror, swore at the madness he was confronted with. Branca attempted to push himself away, back into the press of two men who'd followed him in.

Genner's voice rumbled through the stunned, captivated room. 'We all been expectin' you, Pike. Wanted to make sure you'd finished me, eh?' Genner swept his arm around him. 'Well, I'm livin' to see you hang, you murderin' son of a bitch.' The rancher steadied himself and his eyes sought out Amy. He lifted his voice 'You know it, but hear *me* tell it, lady,' he said.

'Nobody likes to be wrong . . . least of all me. Pike's been pushin' you people around even before he murdered old Smiles.' Genner gave an almost imperceptible nod to Amy. 'Yeah I knew it,' he said meaningfully, then his unsteady gaze turned to Huck.

'I been wrong before, son . . . done lots o' bad things . . . had to. But I never told Pike to do more'n keep an eye on 'em. Get your friends to stop him . . . stop him, before . . .'

Genner's life was ebbing away and his legs collapsed. Lenny and Huck stepped in and supported his great weight, eased him gently to the floor.

That was the signal for the stalemate to end. For the two JUG punchers stood behind Branca, there had only ever been one boss. They shoved a little, but Branca was fractionally ahead of them. He used his left hand to pull a Colt, pushed the barrel of that and his rifle into their bodies. 'You'll never get to spend your pay if you do,' he threatened.

As Branca forced his way on to the veranda, Amy and Huck paid heed to Lenny's silent gesturing for them to remain still. He knew their ammunition was all but finished and wanted to see the outcome; if the men formed new ranks, what Branca and Furloe Stilt did next. He exchanged his Colt with Huck's Winchester. The youngster shook his head, held up four, then five fingers – his estimate of the number of remaining bullets.

Most of the men who'd been hired by Branca to fight realized they'd been duped into an unpromising future. They'd never been up for head-to-head gunplay and their skirmish ended in confusion with threats, curses and clumsy grappling.

No one paid much attention to Branca and Stilt. But Lenny was watching. He leaped to the ground and parried a fist, lashed out with the barrel of the rifle. Trying to see where Branca had gone, he side-stepped the tangle of flailing bodies, wondered where Stilt was skulking. With his broken face, he'd be the one who'd done for Rio.

Like Genner, Lenny was no killer, no murderer. But

now, standing alone, it was kill or be killed. Stilt might turn away, but Branca – never.

He looked towards the broken gate that led from the yard to the west pasture; with his teeth he dragged his glove tight on his left hand. As Stilt walked towards him he tried not to flinch as the bullet seared his left shoulder.

'Too many misses,' Lenny called out, as one bullet from his Winchester tore away the left side of Stilt's face. For a moment, Lenny saw the stark white of exposed bone, before the wash of blood. It didn't put Stilt down though. He stumbled, threw up his hands to try and hold the blood that gushed from his shattered face. But then as he buckled, Lenny shot him again. 'That's from Rio,' he snarled, and put a bullet high in the man's chest. It sent Stilt into the dust, his blood soaking the ground in big, sinister stains.

Lenny heard Huck shout and he swung round, just as someone appeared from the back corner of the house. Branca had got hold of a shotgun, and he grasped it in white-knuckled hands. Lenny continued to move, lunged forward and down, dropping below the level of the twin muzzles. He heard the great blast of sound as one barrel exploded, felt the hot wind as the shot wailed over his head, He hit the ground, his body jarring from the shock. He brought the Winchester up, firing off a shot low in Branca's belly. The man screamed as the bullet ripped deep into his body, howled long and shrill at the impact against muscle then bone.

'Old Smiles Macaw never made as much fuss as that,' Lenny said bitterly.

Branca fell back against the lean-to, but despite his dreadful wound managed to retain his grip on the shotgun. As he saw Lenny come to his feet, he jerked his finger back against the second trigger. The shotgun roared again, spat a gout of flame and smoke. Lenny felt the burning rasp across his side, then the swamp of warm blood run to his thigh. He swore, swung the Winchester in a short curve and pointed the muzzle at Branca's head. He pulled the trigger, heard the dull click as the hammer fell against an empty chamber. But he didn't move. He just stood his ground for the time it took the man to die.

Lenny dropped the rifle, slowly turned to the front door of the house. With a smile, he sarcastically held up three fingers to Huck who was standing there with Amy.

It was as Lenny was considering the folly of any further move, that both Amy and Huck shouted. They were pointing at the riders who were approaching from west of the wagon road: the riders whom Lenny assumed were coming to finish off what Branca and his men had started.

The rising sun glinted on the silver star that was pinned to the first man into the yard, and Lenny blinked. But it wasn't the badge or the assuredness with which Porton Gane rode that wound up Lenny. It was the lean unshaven faces of the men following. The slouch hats and dusty garb that hollered a trail drive; a trail drive from the Wyoming–Colorado border.

'The herd!' rasped Lenny, and looked closely at the group of punchers. One of them walked his cow pony slowly forward. He was slumped in the saddle and the brim of his hat was pulled low. He was bandaged and dirty, but unmistakably Rio.

'Jesus, I thought you were dead. We all thought you were dead,' Lenny shouted, laughed, as he rushed forward. 'The moro came back . . . with Stilt,' Lenny continued as he reached up to help Rio swing down. 'Where you been . . . you got to Billings?'

'He never made it to the nearest town,' drawled the ramrod who sauntered up to them. 'Seems to have spent most of one night playin' games with some long-range shootist.'

'Furloe Stilt,' Lenny said.

'Yeah,' Rio agreed. 'You forgot to warn me about him. After he shot me I got deep into the trees. I wasn't hurt bad, but, I lost the moro to him. I figured I'd make Fishtail on foot . . . the JUG maybe . . . get me another mount. But I must o' passed out. The next thing I know it's early mornin' and my head's full o' cattle noise. The first person I see when I'm out of the trees is the sheriff. He's ridin' alongside Muff, with our herd.'

Lenny looked at the ramrod who offered to shake hands. 'Muff Dublin' he said. 'We'd made it to Billings . . . were bedded down,' he explained. 'Mr Gane heard we were headin' for Elk Valley and rode out to look us over. When he finds out who we are . . . where we're goin', he says he'll come along . . . one or two things to sort out.' Dublin spat a thin stream of black juice. 'After we met up with Rio, we put the herd into a run. They're no more than an hour behind. Some o' the boys don't like to miss a fight, Mr Sand.'

Lenny looked around him. 'We've just had it,' he said. 'If they want some fun they can ride into Fishtail. I reckon they might pick up some scatterlin's on the way . . . some as need brandin'.' He winked at Rio.

His brother chuckled. 'An' look out for Lenny's stallion.' He rubbed his side, saw Stilt lying dead on the ground. 'He had it comin'. Him an' Branca both. I'm jus' sorry I wasn't here to help you, brother,' he said wearily.

Lenny began to say something, but stopped when the sheriff came out of the house. Gane spoke quietly, and a more aware, grown-up-looking Huck Genner went back inside with Amy.

Gane stepped down into the yard, walked over to Lenny. 'Genner's lost his grip. He never went a happy man . . . but he told me what's been happenin'. Dyin' man's statement . . . you know. I guess most things're sorted now.'

Lenny and Rio looked at each other. 'Yeah, most things,' Lenny said. 'Now if you'll ride with me, Sheriff, we'll go get Dub. He needs to be back home.'

Lenny took the reins of the pony Rio had been riding. As he mounted, he looked back at the house and Amy was in the doorway. She knew what he was doing, where he was going and she waved quickly.

It was the second time Lenny had experienced the feeling. This time, he *knew* he liked her.

'If this is all over, maybe we'll get that dance hall in town,' Rio said, looking up at his brother. 'What're you after, Lenny?' he asked.

'That garden of Eden I once saw here. That an' all the trimmins'.'